Awake when all the world is asleep

Awake when all the world is asleep

stories

Shree Ghatage

Published in 1997 by
House of Anansi Press Limited
1800 Steeles Avenue West, Concord, ON
Canada L4K 2P3

Distributed in Canada by
General Distribution Services Inc.
30 Lesmill Road
Toronto, Canada   M3B 2T6
Tel. (416) 445-3333
Fax (416) 445-5967
e-mail: Customer.Service@ccmailgw.genpub.com

01 00 99 98 97   1 2 3 4 5

CATALOGUING IN PUBLICATION DATA
Ghatage, Shree
Awake when all the world is asleep
ISBN 0-88784-602-5
I. Title.
PS8563.H37A82 1997   C813'.54   C97-931855-6
PR9199.3.G42A82 1997

Cover design: Pekoe Jones
Printed and bound in Canada
Typesetting: ECW Type & Art, Oakville

*House of Anansi Press gratefully acknowledges the support
of the Canada Council for the Arts and the
Ontario Arts Council for our publishing program.*

For my parents, Dada and Manjootai Modak,
& Tai,
who are always with me

CONTENTS

Conqueror of cities, young seer,
Born with unlimited power,
The Spirit sustains every act . . .

— Hymn to Indra, the Embodied Spirit
Rig Veda 1.11.4

Awake when all the world is asleep

Heaven-Earth Difference

Throughout the long flight home, staring out a pin-hole window, watching deep night become gold, blue, mustard, black again, I thought about my parents and how I was going to tell them about Simon and my decision to immigrate to Canada. They'd met him the previous summer when they'd visited me in Winnipeg, but only as a friend. I felt a certain sadness for them now: because of the permanent distance my decision was going to put between us, because it had always been the plan that after all my studying was finished I would join Dad in his practice in Bombay.

The first time I saw Simon I was in the library reading *Williams Obstetrics* and he was huddled over a telescope, outside. It was the coldest night of the year and the moon was so new that the brightest objects in the sky were the distant constellations. I dozed off staring at his glowing snowsuit, wondering how much longer he would be able to stay out there. When I opened my eyes, he was sitting in the armchair opposite me. He smiled, and pointing to the tiny diamond in my left nostril, asked, "How does that stay in place?" I wondered whether he had been waiting for me to wake up just so he could ask that question.

"It'll be easier if I show it to you," I said. I carefully pulled out the diamond and, after wiping it on my handkerchief, laid it on his open palm. He examined the mechanism then looked up at me and asked, "Where in India are you from?"

My time in Winnipeg had been lonely; his curiosity caught me by surprise.

"I'm sorry, I'm Simon Roberts," he said. "I'm writing a thesis on applied geometry and trigonometry." He pointed to the telescope at his feet.

"I'm Shaila Goray," I said. "I'm from Bombay." I opened my hand for the diamond.

"How long have you been in Winnipeg?" he asked.

"I came in '68. Which makes it two years, and a half."

"And how much longer before you'll be licensed to deliver babies unassisted?" He pointed to my textbook.

I smiled. "One and a half if I pass both my exams."

I loved Simon for his hundred and one questions, for the mossy riverbed of his eyes, for his ability to reduce the universe to graceful parabolas, exquisitely balanced equations, flowing curves.

Never in my life had I worn so many skins as when I lay on my back next to him, covered in layers of clothing under a down-filled suit, the nearness and warmth from his body radiating into mine. I looked through his telescope at stars yellow, red, blue, noticing how greatly they differed in their brightness. And sometimes, if I focused my eyes long enough on one spot, the stars would blur and the spaces between would assume shapes. While Simon pointed out the constellations, I would call out the landscape of the sky: the steeply rising curve of a swan's neck, high mountains peaking in a cupped hand, angled wings of a hawk lifting off the ground.

Once, he told me, "You're making them up, Shaila, all those shapes. You're imagining them."

"Exchange places," I said, plucking at his sleeve, "hold your head exactly the way I am holding mine." He laughed and pulling me on top of him, tugged on the zipper of my jacket.

"First things first," I said, "move over." I directed his gaze eastward. "See that seven-finger lake?"

He stared hard for a moment then reached for my zipper again. And later, when I searched the sky behind the wavy silhouette of his head, the lake had disappeared and all I could see were the stars.

The airplane descended quickly and my mounting queasiness gathered at the pit of my stomach. As we came closer to ground level, what had seemed like burning torches became the cooking fires of hutment dwellers whose homes line the periphery of Bombay's Santa Cruz Airport. As soon as the heavy doors of the airplane opened, the strong aromas of frying curry leaves, roasting brinjal, and pungent garam masala cleared my head of all previous thoughts, and suddenly I was impatient for the shikeykai smell of Mum's wiry hair, for the bitter taste of raw beetlenut that Dad often carried in his pocket.

The immigration queue was quick. The customs officer wore a sleeveless woollen sweater, its variegated brown stripes hugging his narrow chest like a tight bandage; I supposed it protected him from the blast of fans that were turning at high speed everywhere. He pointed to the camera case around my neck and asked, "What is that?"

"A camera," I said, "to take photographs of my father's sixtieth birthday."

"No selling camera when in India," he admonished. "You are understanding this?" I nodded; his look told me I had understood nothing.

I saw my parents before they saw me. They were talking animatedly with two young men, one of whom pointed in my

5

direction. Mum and Dad turned and waved and smiled at me. We rushed towards each other and hugged. Mum stroked my hair away from my face. Dad ran his hand over my back.

Dad beckoned the two men to our side. "Shaila, meet Arun and Arjun Joshi. They live on the fifth floor, just below us." My parents had moved into Maya Building the previous year, and I'd gathered from Mum's detailed letters about her new neighbours that she and Dad had become well-acquainted with most of them. I smiled at the twin brothers with identical laughing mouths, and one of them — the less shy one — lifted my suitcases and carried them to the car. The other held open the door for me.

"What do you think of them?" Mum asked, as soon as we were on our way. "Their father is coming in on Singapore flight. They're a lawyer family." Her voice was affectionate, spiked with enthusiasm.

"How come one of them recognized me?" I asked.

"Oh! everyone has seen your photographs in our sitting room. What do you think of them?" she asked again, smiling.

"I barely said hello, Mum."

"But still," she insisted.

"Why don't you simply tell her?" Dad glanced at Mum.

"Tell me what?" I said.

"They're good boys," Mum turned around in her seat so she could face me. "Your father and I thought that maybe, *if* you like one of them, you could get engaged —"

"You're kidding!" I said.

"What?" Dad said.

"You can't be serious. You want me to get engaged just like that!"

"You are here a fortnight," Mum said. "Meet them during that time. Decide before you leave. You have six months to complete your studies. It would be nice if you could get engaged

6

now. Simple exchange of rings. When you return, we can have wedding. What?"

I was shaking my head. "I can't get engaged," I said. "I've been applying for gynecology positions all over Canada for after I'm finished."

Mum turned and faced front. A passing shower sprinkled our car with thick drops of rain.

"Why didn't you write as soon — ?" Dad's voice was stern.

"Because I wanted to tell you in person, that's why." Anger the size of a fist was clogging my throat, flattening my voice, making it alien to my ears.

"What is there in Canada that is not here?" Dad insisted.

"Experience —"

"If experience is what you want, Shaila," Mum said, "you don't have to work with your father right away." She turned to Dad. "She could work with Bankim Nath in Calcutta, couldn't she, or K.K. Moorthy in Bangalore?"

"There you go again, Mum, deciding where I should work, who I should marry." I rolled down the window; the fishy stench of Mahim Causeway rushed in like a tidal wave.

"When do you think you will have had enough of this so-called experience?" Dad asked with calm control.

"I don't know. I'm still in the job-applying stage. Let me decide on where I want to be. Begin working. I'll be able to tell you after that."

"Are you saying you may not want to come back?" Mum's intuition never failed her.

"That's possible," I said.

"Your cousin Ramesh said the same thing when he came home from Manchester," Dad said. "Someone offered him a job in an engineering firm there. The foolish boy accepted. Then he came home and your uncle suggested he go for a few

7

interviews and before you know it, he has a job. Company has not provided flat yet. But company Fiat is at his disposal. Only a matter of time before he gets his own flat and car-driver."

I shook my head.

Mum pulled her sari around her right shoulder and dabbed her eyes with it. Her movements were compact, contained.

And I hadn't even told them about Simon yet.

I rolled up the window. The fresh, earth-scented breeze blowing off the rain-drenched city was more than I could bear.

I sat on the divan on the verandah reading. The coconut fronds undulating against a blue sky reminded me of the stiff winds and battering snow that had almost prevented my reaching Winnipeg Airport seven days earlier. The hot air settled on me like a moist blanket and I felt safe and comfortable in its familiarity. This is where a part of me belongs, I thought, stretched out on my back, Dad's leather-bound Somerset Maugham in my hands; here, where the once-white pedestal fan clatters noisily, dispelling cooled, moisture-packed heat.

Mum came out to join me and I moved over so she could sit down. She held out a plate of semolina ladoos and briefly ran her hands over my calves. Ever since our conversation in the car, neither she nor Dad had brought up the subject of meeting boys again. I had gone with Dad to his maternity home a few times, but when he suggested that I go on rounds with him, Mum shook her head and said I needed a rest. She prepared my favourite dishes, took me shopping, asked questions about Winnipeg, the hospital, the few friends she had met, remembering their names with remarkable accuracy. Simon's she must have forgotten because she never mentioned him. Regrettably, because it would have provided an opportunity to bring him into the conversation.

I bit into the semolina ladoo. "It's delicious, Mum," I said. "How are the preparations coming along?" The following day was the party for Dad's sixtieth birthday. Mum had planned a thanksgiving Satya Narayan puja to Lord Vishnu followed by lunch for relatives and friends.

"Fine," she nodded. "I've been thinking, Shaila. You're coming home after a long time: why don't you sit for the puja along with your father and me?"

We had performed family pujas in the past. The last time I'd sat for one was before I'd left for Winnipeg; special prayers had been offered so that the gods would grant me speedy success. It seemed a long time ago.

"All right," I said. I had stopped believing in rituals some time ago but I supposed a few prayers wouldn't hurt.

Dad came out on the verandah. "Have you sent Bayabai to the market?" he asked Mum. "I have an early clinic and I want tea."

"I've sent her to buy some fresh fruit for tomorrow," Mum said, standing up. "I'll make tea for all of us."

"So, Shailu, what are you going to wear tonight?" Dad asked.

"We're not going out, are we?"

He nodded. "The Joshis have invited us for dinner. I'm surprised your mother didn't tell you."

"You go. I'm feeling exhausted. Tell them I still have jet lag or something." I did feel tired.

"But this evening was planned for you, Shaila. Arun and Arjun will be there. Ask your mother," Dad said as she came back out.

"I don't want to ask anyone anything," I said. "I thought I had made it very clear that I wasn't interested in —"

"We're not forcing you, Shaila. Just meet them —" Dad said.

9

"You haven't done something utterly ridiculous like prom-ised me to one of them, have you?" I couldn't hold back my tears.

"No," Mum's voice was smooth, reasonable. "Mrs. Joshi and I discussed the possibility of making a match long before you arrived. She suggested we arrange a meeting. That's all."

"I'm not going," I said, turning my head and wiping my eyes.

"Yes you are. We won't cancel last minute." Dad sounded angry. I saw Mum shake her head at him.

"I cancelled tonight's dinner the day after you arrived, Shaila. I told Mrs. Joshi that you were staying on indefinitely in Canada and there wouldn't be much use —"

"I can't believe all this has been happening behind my back," I said, standing up, my book dropping to the floor.

I could still hear Mum and Dad talking from inside my room. Dad raised his voice. "I think it's high time you convinced Shaila. So what if she gets tearful. She needs to be told that whatever we're suggesting is for her own good."

I could imagine Mum shaking her head. She spoke softly but I heard her say, "The world has changed since you and I were married. Girls want independence to choose their own partners these days. The more you force her the more stub-born she will become. After all, remember, she's your daughter through and through. I *will* talk to her . . ."

I lay down and looked through the window at the darkening sky. I wished Simon could have come with me; we would have watched nightfall together. The arrangement of the stars was so different here.

When Simon and I weren't watching the stars, I would lie on his bed, practising tying my surgical knots onto his pillowcase. Sometimes, he would kneel next to me and hold out his notebook filled with freehand figures so neatly drawn that their precision would take my breath away. Once, he drew tumbling buildings made of rhomboids, ellipses, lozenges, kites, crooked houses lining angled streets; his page a city without a point of reference. "Which is the north, which is the south? The east, the west?" I asked, pointing to an untidy monument in the corner.

He turned off the light and brushing my face with his mouth, murmured, "Here an arc, here two, a cupid's bow," he moved down, "two miniature cones, concave dip, inverted pyramid . . ." Afterwards, he turned to me and said, "Apply for immigration, Shaila. There are lots of jobs. Canada's a growing nation. Pacific to Atlantic. Take your pick . . ." He spoke quickly, much too quickly for him.

"What are you really trying to say?" I asked, looking past him at the large oak whose shadow was shifting course. Soon, the footpaths would be strewn with leaves.

"That's right," Dad said, walking into the room, "ask whether he will be able to provide you the same kind of life that Arun and Arjun would . . . does he even have a job? How is it no one can tell us a thing about his family —"

"Why before marriage, Shaila?" Mum was saying, covering my bareness with a soft mulmul sari.

"I don't want you to leave," Simon interlaced his fingers in mine. "That's all. Nothing more, nothing less. Don't want you to leave —" I opened my eyes. The windowpane was dark. Downstairs, a caged parrot was squawking. I turned in bed looking for Simon and heard Mum calling out to me that dinner was ready.

Only a week ago, at the airport, Simon had said, "We should look for a job in the same city when you get back, Shaila, so we can get married afterwards. What do you think?"

I had looked at him in disbelief. "Why are you springing this on me now, just when I'm boarding a flight?"

"Because I love you. You must have known that this is where our relationship was heading —"

"Why now, Simon? Why choose this moment? We don't even have the time to discuss —"

"I didn't think there was anything to discuss. I was going to ask you after you came back but seeing you just now — I just don't want to lose you to an arranged marriage —"

"An arranged marriage, Simon? That's preposterous! What are you thinking? That I will be manipulated against my will?"

"I'm not saying that at all. I know how different things are in India, and telling your parents about me won't be easy and they may persuade you to —"

"Nothing like that is going to happen. I have to go now, that's the last boarding call. I've left my flight number and time of arrival next to your bed. See you in a few weeks," I said, adjusting my backpack.

"You *are* going to tell them about me, aren't you?" he asked. But I was already walking through security.

Bayabai opened my bedroom door and a warm smell of bubbling jaggery on a hot griddle entered the room. "Mother sent me to call you. Come quickly while gule poli is still fresh."

I sat for the puja with Mum and Dad the next morning. Dense, fragrant smoke snaked towards the ceiling as the priest fed the lit crucible with camphor-pebbles, read from the Pothi devotional descriptions of Lord Vishnu, and chanted prayers. I added yellow roses to sage leaves, jasmine, and frangipane flowers that covered the shaligram in a growing heap. We repeated mantras, Mum, Dad, and I, our voices braiding to-gether in tight harmony.

Mum's cooking was inspired on Dad's birthday. Many relatives came, some of whom I hadn't seen for several years; suddenly my three years away seemed like nothing and I forgot I was leaving for Winnipeg in a week's time. My cousins thanked me repeatedly for setting a family precedent by going abroad for my post-graduation. And my aunts and uncles commented on how fair and fetching I had become now that I'd lost all my tan; they predicted there would be zero difficulties in finding me a boy.

Late in the afternoon, the Maya Building neighbours were gathered around listening to Arun and Arjun animatedly describing an octogenarian granduncle who had been checking his pulse for half a century now because a face reader had once told him that he wouldn't survive middle age. Everyone was laughing. Saroj Atya, Mum and Dad's neighbour from the fifth floor, saw me standing in the doorway and patted the armrest of the sofa, "Come and sit down, Shaila, you look tired."

I smiled and pushed my hair away from my forehead but stayed where I was.

"So, Shaila!" Saroj Atya dispersed several winks around the room, "did Arun and Arjun take you to see the latest Rajesh Khanna film or not?"

I looked at Dad; he was smiling.

But Saroj Atya wasn't finished. She winked again, "Both brothers are too good, I tell you. You will have to do eenie meenie mynie mo —"

"Actually, Saroj Atya," Arjun — the less shy one — interrupted, "we've already seen the latest Rajesh Khanna film. We did think of asking Shaila whether she would like to come with us to the law courts. We're pleading property cases. However, since she is busy meeting old friends we thought she would have no time for domestic disputes." His tone was level, matter-of-fact, and I think he deliberately spoke at length.

Grateful, I flashed a vague smile in Arjun's direction.

Obviously the whole Maya Building now knew about Mum and Dad's attempts at matchmaking and I was furious. Without a word I turned and went to the kitchen looking for Mum.

"Shaila," Dad said, walking in, "if I had known that sending you to Winnipeg would end up in you behaving rudely with our guests —"

"And if I had known I would be so humiliated perhaps I wouldn't even have come home!"

My first two years in Winnipeg, I used to pretend I was a snail. If a snail can carry its home wherever it goes, I'd reason, then so can I. Lying in my bed, painstakingly coiling the essence of everything I valued into the shell on my back, I would fall asleep, knowing that home wasn't distant but here, with me. Then, responding to Simon's insatiable curiosity, and afterwards to the ardent, familiar nearness of him, I found myself unburdening until what was inside was exposed and the yearning I felt for everything that was far away became bearable.

Now here I was, at home, folding into my shell not only Simon, but the freedom and independence that allowed me to exercise my will without censure, without the interference of tradition and mores. When I was in Winnipeg all I needed to feel complete was home, and now that I was home I felt incomplete without Simon. It was as though home and Simon could not coexist.

After everyone left, Mum insisted that Dad lie down for a while. He took the newspaper from the shoe stand and told Bayabai to call him when it was time for dinner. I went out onto the verandah where two crows were perched on the side ledge,

14

heads tucked into their necks, beady eyes roving. Mum came and joined me.

"There is something you are not telling us," she said.

"It's Simon —"

"Your friend in Winnipeg?"

"Well, he's more than a friend. In fact he's part of the reason I want to stay on in Canada."

"Has he received his doctorate in mathematics or not?"

I looked at her. "He's asked me to marry him," I said.

She didn't say anything.

"We're going to look for jobs in the same place when I return. Shouldn't be too difficult but finding the right job in the right place may take a bit of time."

It was a few minutes before Mum spoke. "I knew I was going to lose you one day, Shaila," she said, "but never, not even when I saw you and Simon together in Winnipeg, did I think that you would actually marry someone from another world. Maybe I was hoping that the attraction I saw between you was a passing one. We knew from your letters that you were very lonely." Mum turned to look at me.

"It wasn't just loneliness that drew me to him, Mum! It's more than that," I said.

"In any case," she continued, "I won't tell you what you have no doubt already discovered: there is a zameen-aasmaan pharak, a heaven-earth difference between the East and the West. However, I will say this. Remember, you are not simply a product of your own times where independence and freedom to do as you wish are prized commodities, but the product of generations of people who have lived a particular way of life, subscribed to a particular line of thought for over five thousand years. I want you to think very carefully before you reject this culture which is so much a part of you in order to establish that you — and nobody else — have control over your life."

I was silent. I hadn't expected this reaction. I had been rehearsing a scenario where Dad would tell me in no uncertain terms to dismiss Simon's proposal and return to Bombay as planned, and Mum would diffuse the tension by suggesting that I seek experience in India before working with Dad, with whomsoever and wherever I wished.

"Shaila?" Mum said, "were you listening?"

I nodded. The crows were restless now, opening and closing their wings in little bursts, stretching their necks. Mum left the verandah. I lay down on the divan and opened my book, finding my place easily. When I looked up again, the crows were no longer there; they must have flown away silently because I hadn't heard the flapping of their wings.

Hiru

I

He wouldn't quite admit it to himself but everyone in the village knew that Hiru was a wife-killer.

"What can I do, Bhai? You know my hands are tied!" Hiru said to his cousin after a third wife's remains had been submerged in the tranquil Godavari River. The fumes of the harsh home-brew rose through him, bringing guilt and resolve in equal measure. "I have duty to ancestors — Pawar name cannot die with me. And who will light my funeral pyre when time comes? I need another wife."

Bhai agreed. He upheld every man's solemn duty to perpetuate his family name, for hadn't he produced nine of his own?

"What you say is true, Hiru. No wife, no children!" Bhai balanced a small ribbed glass of tadi on his knee.

"Joshi kismatwala is offering advice again!" Hiru muttered. Leaning his shaved head against a sagging charpai, he watched a ringed moon glide behind a tattered curtain of clouds. "This morning he pulled me aside, right on banks of Godavari, insisted I go to his room — you know, the one where he keeps his books and charts. Then he said, 'Wife, you do not suit, Hiru! Therefore I say, whynot take mistress? Because mistress does not die, she is grateful to you for her life . . . therefore, she rewards you with hot bed! Wait! Your horoscope . . . look here — red mangal is permanent fixture in house of marriage: very bad luck to wife you bring!'"

"So what do you think of kismatwala's advice?" Bhai asked.

"It's not mistress I need! I can have any woman I want and God knows enough want me. But truly cousin, wife is wife, is she not?"

Bhai grunted vaguely.

"Bichara badnaseeb," he commiserated silently with Hiru. "Never lived long enough with wife or he'd know answer to question. Now take my own, Charu. I haven't looked at another pair of anklets in all married years, but is that enough? Better not ask. All she thinks is food or rather, shortage of it. Ten stomachs to feed, she reminds me night and day . . . what about my stomach, I want to ask her, shouldn't you say eleven stomachs? Instead I try to persuade, 'Whynot have operation, Charu? Doctor guarantees no more children after that!' But she gets angry, 'Whynot *you* have operation — Doctor says much better that man have operation!' Then what does she do? Freezes me out, for whole month, from menses to menses. Every time I ask for hot milk, my own, private signal to indicate desire to share her bed, she mutters, 'Stove isn't stoked — it'll have to be cold milk tonight.' And goes into inner room, unrolls bedding, surrounds herself with the nine of them so I can't even plead with her. But why tell Hiru all this, bichara badnaseeb, in same chakkar again, same conundrum —"

Hiru let out a guttural snore. Bhai drained his tadi and looked upwards. "I thank you, Great Oblivion, Emperor of Panaceas," he shouted, "for taking my cousin under your shadow-less wing!" The sky was dark now, the moon having sought shelter behind some hilly clouds.

It was a similar night, the ringed moon making capricious appearances in a shifting sky, when Hiru's mother died at the age of fifty, giving birth to him, her only child. Hiru's father lingered another year, always mourning the loss of his wife, always blaming his son for her death.

After his father's death, Hiru was raised by his mother's sister, Mavshi, who treated Bhai and him equally, like blood brothers. In a village where want and hunger were not uncommon, her generosity saved Hiru from a waywardness that would otherwise have been his lot. In return, Hiru served her with calm devotion: he fetched water from the communal tap situated a mile out of the village, relieved her of the task of moulding dung into flat fuel pies, took complete charge of the ill-tempered milking-goat that was permanently tethered to a peepul tree in the front yard. When the midday sun caused lights to flash in Mavshi's head, he applied a cold compress to her sore eyes, massaged balm into her scalp and neck.

When Hiru was fifteen, he decided he did not want to make a living from the land because it would mean bonding himself to the local jameendaar. Since several villagers had left in search of jobs, Mavshi suggested he do the same.

Hiru was not to return home for three years.

Before he left, Mavshi gave him the address of a second cousin who worked the night shift at a sugar mill in Bombay. His cousin, glad to see him, insisted Hiru share his cot until he could afford a place of his own. He introduced Hiru to everyone in the neighbourhood: the vegetable-sellers who haggled their produce on the footpaths, the mochi who patched shoes and chappals so worn he needed every skill he possessed to make them usable again, the effeminate bangle-seller who occupied a tiny corner of the flower-seller's shop.

The flower-seller was a talkative man and found in Hiru the

perfect listener, the kind who listened without speaking. By observing him at work, Hiru learned how to disguise wilting flowers by first carefully removing their outer petals, then tightly surrounding them with fresh, shining leaves; he noted the subtle difference between appearance and reality as he watched the flower-seller sprinkle rose water on bouquets, to revive their fading scent; and he acquired the geometry of spacing white mogra buds evenly on a string, so that when they bloomed, they spread thick and dense on the garland. Hiru soon started doing odd jobs for the flower-seller; in exchange he was given two meals a day.

One afternoon, Hiru wrapped some garlands in dried leaves and carried them to a sari shop that was celebrating twenty-five years in business. After hanging the rose garlands over the shop's entrance, Hiru went inside to settle the bill. He found the owner, Chaganlal Saheb, attending to a marriage party.

An adolescent girl, plump and pouting, was standing in front of a mirror trying to select a sari by putting several against her, one at a time. Her mother and sisters sat slumped on high stools, offering comments, making suggestions as they fanned themselves with damp handkerchiefs. Chaganlal Saheb stood by, a tight smile on his face. Sweat trickled down his earlobes, splashed onto his wet collar.

After rejecting dozens of saris, the girl eventually narrowed her choice down to two: one, a tumeric yellow with a wide navy-blue border; the other, a sunset-saffron sprinkled with tiny gold stars. It was obvious to those gathered around that the yellow brought out the sallowness in her skin whereas the saffron gave her a healthy, bride-like glow.

Seeing she was undecided, Hiru came forward. Taking the saffron sari from the floor, he unfolded it and deftly pleating its five-and-a-half-yard length, motioned for the girl to face the mirror. He draped it around her, careful not to touch any part of her body. When he was satisfied that every fold was in place, he stood back. The girl twirled around, laughed at her flattering reflection, insisted Hiru help her with the rest of her selection.

Chaganlal Saheb offered Hiru a job, which he gratefully accepted.

Hiru held a certain disdain for salesmen who flattered or harangued their customers into making purchases. He preferred to let his fingers speak for him. He touched rough handloom as though it was soft mulmul, he stroked cotton as if it were silk, he treated silk with the respect due to gold brocade. He was an aesthete at heart, his efforts to find his client the perfect sari, tireless. Soon, customers started relying on his judgement and came to him when it was time to make the final choice.

The first time he went back to the village, Hiru carried with him a large bundle of rejects from the shop which he handed over to Mavshi to distribute as she thought fit.

His aunt was very happy to see him; she had missed his company, his quiet support. Bhai now had a wife, a child, with another prominently on its way.

Now that he was earning some money, Mavshi suggested Hiru get married. When he told her that he shared a room with three others, that separate quarters for him and his family were simply unaffordable, she said, "Has that ever stopped other villagers from marrying? Do what they all do. Get married and leave your wife here, with us." But Hiru was adamant. He did not want to presume on Mavshi's hospitality any longer; besides, Bhai's family was growing.

Wanting to see him settled soon, Hiru's aunt came up with a compromise. She looked around for a suitable girl and arranged matters in such a way that after the wedding, Hiru's wife would remain behind, in her parents' home.

"You are married man now, Hiru, you have responsibility!" Mavshi reminded him before he left for Bombay. "Don't be forgetting to send your in-laws monthly money order for wife's boarding and lodging."

"I won't forget, Mavshi! I know you've given your word! Besides, she's my wife, isn't she?" Hiru laughed.

Hiru was eighteen on his wedding day, his wife fifteen.

Six months later he was a widower.

It happened like this: One morning, feeling the urge to drink fresh coconut juice, his wife tucked the bottom of her sari into the waist of her petticoat and climbed the coconut tree that stood in her parents' backyard. She plucked several coconuts and threw them down one by one. No sooner had she started her descent, than the black-beaded mangalsutra dangling from her neck reminded her of Hiru. It was unseemly that a married woman show her legs. She began to unloose the bottom of her sari from the waist of her petticoat and in doing so lost her grip. She was dead when they found her, head resting on a rock, ripe coconuts scattered around her like stone petals.

Hiru's second wife had been chopping wood for fuel when the blade of the axe cut her finger. She washed the wound carefully with running water and applied pressure on it until the bleeding stopped. Then she went to the fields for the planting season; the soil was severely infected. Soon afterwards, she developed a sore throat which made it difficult to swallow. Fleeting pains in the neck and back became continuous spasms. Exhaustion and starvation followed, and before long, she was dead. They had been married two years.

Four years after Hiru's third marriage, malaria came to the village. Several villagers died. When Hiru's wife developed a high temperature marked by chills and rigours he was informed immediately. He took leave from the shop, nursed her day and night, but she lapsed into a coma, passed away.

"Now here I am, three wives to my name, yet no issue to carry on family name," Hiru thought when he opened his eyes. A dull, pre-dawn glow suffused the sky. He looked at Bhai who was sitting on the charpai, his hands holding a cup of tea.

Bhai said, "Why don't you take Parvati, Hiru? No one is willing to marry poor girl!" Polio, contracted at a young age, had left Parvati severely crippled in one leg. Hiru nodded and asked Bhai to find an auspicious date for the wedding.

Like a black kohl spot lovingly applied to the cheek of a newborn by its mother in the attempt to distract the heavens' jealousy from the perfection she sees in her little one, Hiru hoped that Parvati's ugly, twisted foot would be the imperfection that would this time keep heaven's envy at bay.

Five years passed, five uneventful years. "I have paid my debt to Fate!" Hiru exulted, when Parvati was with child.

A drenching peace settled on him when, holding his newborn for the first time, Hiru felt her bones dovetail into the crook of his arm. He wondered at her black eyes, so earnest and crossed; he breathed in her fresh scent of tumeric, besan, and milk. He touched her delicate matchstick fingers and forgot that girls are not allowed to perform last rites for their fathers, forgot that they marry and move away.

He told Parvati that he would find suitable accommodation for all of them in town. Parvati smiled, nodded assent. But even as they were making plans for the future, blood was slowly leaking out of her open womb and with it her life.

This time the village drowned itself in tadi for two days.

After yet another foray to the Godavari River, Hiru headed

back to town, leaving his in-laws in charge of Harini, so named because her large eyes, luminous and moist, reminded him of a forest haran, a deer.

Aji and Ajoba, Harini's grandparents, cared for her with a deep love which was selfless because it contained within it a certain element of wise detachment. Hiru came to see her every chance he could get, and Harini would wait for him at the dust-lined bus station every Saturday night. With the passing years, she resembled him more and more; she had his wide face, his calm eyes, his low, fruity chuckle. Seeing them together Aji, not without a tinge of jealousy, would smile at Ajoba and say, "Blood is thicker than water. Once son-in-law's child always son-in-law's child!"

Aji and Ajoba owned a tailor's shop and the day Harini was old enough to know she should keep away from the pointed scissors and distance herself from the coal iron, she was given free reign of it. Ajoba was a perfectionist, a strict task-master and under his tutelage Harini, at first playful and inattentive, became an adequate seamstress. When Ajoba's memory began to waiver, causing him to jumble accounts which he stored in his head, Harini, the only one in her family to go to school, became his accountant. Hiru bought her a ledger from town and she would enter into it the business of the day.

One blazing evening in summer, when Harini had gone with her friends to bathe in a nearby well, Hiru said to Aji and Ajoba, "Do you remember me telling you about Dadaji, driver of Chaganlal Saheb's car? He passed away last month. His widow came to see me at shop. Dadaji's only son, Raju, is of marriageable age — she wants Harini for him, said Dadaji had suggested they have look at Harini for Raju. Imagine! Boy's side coming to me! I said I would talk to you before giving answer. What do you think?"

If Harini had not been so shy on her wedding day, she would have noticed that her bridegroom — whom she simply thought of as Rajuji, BCom (Diploma), son of Dadaji — had smooth skin, narrow hips, soft mannerisms.

Although Sasubai, Harini's mother-in-law, had a careworn, emaciated appearance, her smile, when she thought it fit to bestow, was not unattractive. She liked Harini but was careful to keep her feelings to herself. Sasubai's only outward sign of approval was made when she presented Harini with a thin gold jewellery set on her wedding day.

The villagers smiled and nodded their heads, thumped Hiru on his back.

II

Raju held the post of accountant's assistant in Chaganlal Saheb's sari shop. The very next day, after mother, son, and new daughter-in-law arrived in town, Raju went back to work.

He left at eight in the morning, put in a twelve-hour day. Sasubai, who worked as a supervisor in an orphanage, left soon afterwards and returned at five o'clock in the evening.

Their flat, consisting of two rooms, a kitchen, and a bathroom, was situated on the top floor of a dilapidated building. The kitchen and bathroom overlooked a crowded street with shops at ground level and residential flats above. The front rooms were really one room which had been made into two by the erection of a thin wooden partition in its centre. Consequently, the rooms which had been quite adequate for mother and son afforded no privacy for the young couple. Raju and Harini's embraces in the dark night were therefore hurried and flavourless.

And so their embraces would have continued to be had not Raju forgotten to take his tiffin to work one morning. Since the shop closed for two hours every afternoon, Raju decided to go home for lunch. He entered the flat to find Harini sitting in the kitchen window, her chin resting on drawn-up knees, her gaze fixed on the street below. Raju walked towards her, the noises from the street no longer muffling his footsteps. Startled, Harini stumbled to her feet, her upper-lip damp with perspiration. She wore a sari petticoat; a thin, wet cotton pancha covered her shoulders. She blushed when she realized who it was.

Raju was not prepared for what he saw: her waist so narrow that he could circle it with his two hands, her breasts so small that they appeared to peak in two plump raisins, her lower limbs outlined by the sun so fragile that he was reminded of sap-filled veins of neem leaves. A tawny flush suffused her skin when she reached out for her clothes. He took them from her, caught her against his chest.

That afternoon Raju was late getting back to work.

From that day forward, he came to her every lunch hour and Harini would wait for him, at first timid and anxious, then eager; afterwards, unabashedly impatient.

With tacit, mutual consent they kept their afternoons a secret from Sasubai. Raju took his lunch with him every morning and gave it to a beggar at noon; every evening they pretended not to have seen each other all day long.

Even though the days were oppressive now, the occasional gust of wind carried on its back a tantalizing whiff of moist earth. The monsoons were approaching. One morning when Sasubai told Raju that her umbrella needed repair, Raju said he would get it fixed for her.

A few evenings later, Sasubai noticed the repaired umbrella propped up in the front entrance. Later that night she said, "I saw the umbrella, son . . . you must have brought it home when sari shop closed at midday."

Caught off-guard, Raju looked at Harini. "Yes . . . yes, at midday . . . I forgot . . . piece of paper with address of one delivery . . . came home and dropped it off."

Sasubai saw Harini's flushed face, heard Raju's muttered explanation and the gorge rose bitterly in her throat as the smell of their desire for each other twisted sourly in her nostrils. They realized at once that she suspected the nature of that afternoon, that she had only to enquire at the neighbours' to know that he had been coming home every day. Mortified, Harini went to her room. Raju went out muttering he needed fresh air. When he came home at midnight, Sasubai was sitting in the kitchen window, her eyes fixed on its ledge.

He went and lay next to Harini, touched her shoulder. She opened her eyes. They smiled at each other and were soon fast asleep.

Sasubai remained sitting in the kitchen window, rubbing coarsened hands over her calves, thinking how different everything had been right up until Raju was three years old.

That year, although her husband survived a head-on collision with a truck, Sasubai felt she was widowed when Dadaji sustained a permanent injury to his lower abdomen, disabling him from sharing her bed. After a lengthy stay at the hospital he had come home eager and restored, only to be disappointed by this unexpected failure. Embarrassed and diminished, he started sleeping in the front room.

The prospect of a lifetime of lonely nights with vigorous blood still racing through her veins filled Sasubai with terror. One night, when the throb in her was as raw as it was painful, she went to the kitchen, lit a joss stick and, touching its burning tip to the soft inside of her thighs, sought to put out one fire with another. A period of epileptic fits followed which no amount of conventional medicine could cure. Finally, Dadaji went to the medicine man whose consultation room was the footpath outside the railway station. He came back with a sweet-tasting powder. "No more than little pinch . . . take it as soon as room starts to go round and round," Dadaji cautioned Sasubai. "Small pinch or effects may be lethal." But Sasubai did not want Dadaji's medicine; she put it away at the bottom of the wheat bin in the loft in the kitchen.

As the months passed, Sasubai found her equilibrium. She started working at the orphanage because it kept her mind from thinking futile thoughts. Over a period of time she even came to forgive Dadaji for something she knew was not his fault.

But, unknown to her, her frustrated desire lay coiled like an oppressed snake at the bottom of her spine. And now when it reared its ugly, envious head, it would not be subdued.

Unwanted, distorted thoughts began to gnaw at her consciousness. She had found Raju an unspoiled, untouched girl from the village because city girls with their immodest eyes and brazen fashions were not worthy of her son. But here was Harini, not long enough in town to know local bus routes, and already she was like the rest: bold and frivolous, making love like a harlot in the middle of the afternoon. Curse on her, shame on Raju!

Various unusual occurrences alerted Harini to Sasubai's state of mind.

One evening, Harini almost stepped on the vili — a sickle-shaped cutting knife mounted on a board — which Sasubai had deliberately left on the floor without telling her it was there.

But for her sari which got entangled in its spiked wheel, Harini's foot would have been sliced in two.

Another time Harini and Sasubai were hanging washed clothes in the verandah, using long wooden sticks to throw wet garments over the drying wire. Harini collapsed when Sasubai's wooden stick came down on her head. When Raju saw the bloodied, makeshift bandage, he asked what had happened. Sasubai said the stick had slipped from her hands.

Harini lost her youthful looks. Hiru, who visited frequently, became concerned. His daughter would not tell him what was wrong so he spoke to Raju at the shop; Raju said Harini wouldn't tell him anything either. Hiru suggested he take her home to Aji and Ajoba, have her examined by the vaidya who had seen her from birth. Raju nodded and when he brought up the topic with Sasubai, she — who had been so careful to keep up appearances in front of her son — agreed.

One look at her and Aji, with her eyes of a mother, knew that Harini's troubles were in-law troubles. But she could not get her granddaughter to admit to anything. Harini's expression nevertheless was eloquent: What do you want me to say? Has there ever been a man who has sided with his wife in a dispute with his mother? Besides, what difference would it make if you knew the details? Things will be the same tomorrow, same as they were yesterday, same as they are today . . .

Under Aji's care Harini was restored to her old self.

When Raju became restless, Sasubai suggested that he visit Harini in the village; no point bringing her back, she said, health is most important, especially since Harini has yet to bear children. So Raju began to take the long bus journey to Harini as often as he could. But soon that wasn't enough. Soon he wanted her with him all the time. He brought her home.

This time there were no near accidents, no harsh words. Harini was reassured.

Then one day she became ill. She was up all night, retching and heaving until there was nothing left inside her. Raju smiled; a bundle of fresh, green tamarinds, sour and fat, had arrived from the village the previous evening.

"Who told you to eat so many?" he teased.

"Take them away and distribute them in shop. I'll never touch another as long as I live . . ." Harini groaned.

When Sasubai came home from work that evening, Harini was sleeping. Sasubai went to the kitchen, measured out some rice for dinner. She thought she would make onion bhaji, Raju's favourite. As she was mixing the besan and water, the memory of how Dadaji would cool the bhaji for a hungry, impatient Raju by first tearing it, then blowing on it, filled Sasubai with aching nostalgia.

She was caught unawares when Harini came and stood next to her. "I'm feeling very thirsty," Harini said. Sasubai handed her a glass of water.

"I'll get you something hot to drink," she said to her daughter-in-law, leading her back to her room. Sasubai brewed some sweet tea, mixing into it the powder she removed from the bottom of the wheat bin in the loft in the kitchen.

A few hours later Harini was dead.

The government hospital had a shortage of pathologists, a backlog of postmortems. Chaganlal Saheb contacted a police friend who signed the necessary papers for the cremation.

Hiru took Harini's ashes to the village, submerged them in the Godavari River.

Afterwards, he went to Joshi kismatwala, hammered on his door and refusing to put a foot inside that familiar room filled with books and charts, dragged him out on the street. He cursed the bald-headed man for not telling him that the mangal in his horoscope was equally bad for his progeny. "Why did you not warn me?" he croaked, exhausted by sleeplessness and despair.

Bhai tried to lead Hiru away. "Come brother!" he said. "Leave it alone. Who could have predicted this?"

But Joshi kismatwala was calm. This was not the first time he had seen stars manipulate souls like puppets on a string.

"Go home, my son," he said softly. "For guilt there is no need. On this catastrophe your horoscope has no bearing. Just as you were born with your fate, so the beautiful Harini was born with hers."

Hiru returned to the shop but his heart was no longer in his work. When Chaganlal Saheb made him a doorman, he did not protest. Then, to alleviate his gnawing loneliness, to fill the hole that gaped wide within his heart, Hiru did what he could have done a long time ago — he took a mistress instead of another wife. And finally, the guilt and anxiousness that had dogged him his entire life were replaced by the comforting certainty that his next trip to the Godavari River would be his last.

Tara

I was sure adopting Tara was a last-minute decision. Mum didn't call me Cabbage Ears for nothing, yet even I hadn't heard a single word about any adoption until the very night before Tara was to be picked up at Dadar Railway Station.

That night, no matter how much I turned and tossed, I couldn't shake off the heat that covered my body like a heavy counterpane. I called out to Bayabai to fetch me a glass of water and when she didn't answer, I walked out on the balcony that ran along the back of our house. When I heard voices accompanied by a faint clatter of dishes and scraping spoons, I knew Dad was eating a late dinner; I lay down quietly on the divan outside the dining-room window.

"It's decided then. I will fetch Tara from Dadar Station tomorrow afternoon. Would you like Bayabai to make you some buttermilk?" Mum asked, pushing back her chair.

"I'll take curds today," Dad said, "but isn't tomorrow your Samaj afternoon?" He sounded tired. His clinic must have run on longer than usual. I heard his spoon scrape the curds bowl.

"Well, I'll just have to miss my embroidery class," Mum said. "Someone has to fetch the poor girl from the station. Meera Kaku refuses to go, Vinayak Kaka may not be back from his office in time —"

"I thought the whole idea of Vinayak Kaka adopting Tara was so that she would be good company for Meera Kaku. Surely Kaku should go to the station. Why don't you tell her that you will go with her?"

"I already did," Mum said and clicked her tongue. "Anyway, fetching Tara is the least I can do under the circumstances. Now that her grandmother is dead, the poor girl has no one."

"You know that's not true, Anu! I still think Tara should have been sent to her father's brother in Calcutta. This is a crazy scheme on the part of Kaka. I know he's doing it for all the right reasons but you know how Kaka is —"

"Shaila!" Mum's voice was stern, "It's past ten-thirty. You should be fast asleep by now."

I ran back to my room wondering how she knew I was there. I'd taken special care not to be seen, even crawling on my knees when I'd come alongside the dining-room window. But I didn't dwell on that for long for I was too excited about the prospect of having a brand-new relative to play with. My thoughts wandered all over the place: I tried to imagine the unknown Tara's face. Would it be triangular like mine or round like the moon? Everyone said I was tall for my age: would she tower over me or come up to my shoulders? I must have fallen asleep at some point because now Tara was wearing a white frock with a pink collar. She was looking out the window and I was telling her that even though I perfectly understood how very sad and lonely she must feel now that she was all alone in the world, I nevertheless wanted to assure her that Vinayak Kaka and Meera Kaku — although elderly — were kind and good and if any-thing were to happen to my parents tomorrow, I would have Kaka and Kaku for my parents, no problem. I put my arm around her, but when she turned my way I couldn't see her features because they were blurred with tears.

34

Early next morning, I woke to the sound of the milk van clanging to a halt under my bedroom window. I found Mum in the Devghar, doing puja. She'd already had her bath and was laying various flowers at the feet of the gods, keeping the petals in place by applying a dab of sandalwood paste to their base.

"Don't come in, Shaila, without brushing your teeth. Then come back and do namaskar." She didn't look at me, just continued to decorate the gods and resumed chanting her Gayatri Mantra.

"Aum bhoor bhuwa swaha
Tat savitur varenyam
Bhargo devasya dhi mahi
Dhiyo yo na pracho dayata."

The Sun God must have heard her then, for suddenly the sky brightened.

I went to the bathroom, brushed my teeth, and changed into my shorts and blouse, hastily tying a blue sash around my waist. Then I ran to the Devghar, did namaskar, and entered the dining room where Mum was drinking her tea. She poured me some from the teapot and went to the kitchen to fill the rest of my cup with boiled milk. She stirred in two spoonfuls of sugar and placed it in front of me. "It's too white, Mum!" I said, peering inside the cup. "You put too much milk."

She pretended not to hear me, just continued to sip her tea. But she didn't ignore me for long, for soon her face softened and she reached across and stroked my cheeks after smoothing a strand of hair away from my forehead. "I want you to walk home from school this afternoon, Shaila. I have to go to the railway station."

"I know!" I blurted, then put my hand over my mouth.

35

She smiled. "Well, there's no need to tell you more. Here's your father. Come and sit next to me. Give him his chair."

I sat on Dad's lap while Mum went into the kitchen to boil water for a fresh cup. I finished my overly milky tea, then standing behind him, put my arms around his neck. "Sports practice this morning, I see, Shailu," he said, leaning his head briefly against my blouse. "How're the leap frogs and three-legged races coming along?"

"Not bad, Dad. It's heights that make me dizzy —"

"Try and come home early this evening," Mum said to Dad, placing his tea in front of him. "What with all the excitement of Tara arriving, Vinayak Kaka is sure to get breathless." She opened a new packet of Parle Glucose biscuits, put two on his saucer, handed me one.

"Can I come to the station with you, Mum? Please?" I pleaded.

"Only if you get permission from your teacher to miss afternoon periods, Shaila."

"Oh! That's not fair —"

"And why are you already changed? You haven't had your bath yet."

But Mum was too distracted to take me to task, I knew, or else she would have noticed what I was wearing before now. I ran out, shouting, "It's sports practice today. I'll have a bath after school . . ."

By four o' clock that afternoon, I couldn't wait to reach home. I swung open the gate of our bungalow and ran to the kitchen.

"Your mother is at Vinayak Kaka's," Bayabai said. I grabbed a ladoo from a large dish in front of her. Warm semolina melted in my mouth leaving behind a delicious aftertaste of sweet, clarified butter. I ran back from the front door, stuffed another ladoo in my mouth. After nudging off my shoes, I hurriedly got into a pair of chappals and raced across the narrow side lane. I leaned against Vinayak Kaka's front door. It was open.

I hesitated before walking into the sitting room. They must have heard me enter because Mum came to the door and Kaka called out, "Come Shailu, come and meet Tara." I brushed past Mum and threw my arms around Kaka who was sitting in his rocking chair.

"I'm going home now, Shaila. Don't be long. You have homework to do," Mum said.

Kaka was smiling. He pointed towards the window and that's when I saw her. Tara. She was not at all what I'd imagined her to be. She looked sixteen. Her long hair was neatly combed into two plaits and she was wearing a lemon- coloured, nine-yard sari. The lemon colour made her skin look dark.

"What do you think, Shailu?" Kaka said. "Can you and Tara become friends? She's here to stay, you know —"

"You should have changed out of your sports uniform, Shaila," Meera Kaku said, coming out of the kitchen. Her voice was gruff, annoyed.

"She was eager to meet Tara, that's all. Here, Shailu," Kaka turned to me, "Take this to Tara." He handed me the cup of tea that Kaku had just laid on the side table next to him.

"Tara can come to the kitchen," Kaku said, taking the cup from my hands. She laid it on the side table again, walked out of the room.

"I don't know what's gotten into her," Kaka muttered, sipping his tea quickly. I sat on the sofa, tracing the cracks between the mosaic floor tiles with my foot. Nobody said anything as Kaka drained his cup.

"Tara!" Kaka called out from the kitchen. I looked up.

Tara moved away from the window, and as she was picking

up Vinayak Kaka's empty cup, she smiled at me; I grinned. I instantly forgave her for not being my age.

After Tara entered the kitchen, Kaka made a sign for me to sit on his lap. He took my right hand in his, clicked the knuckles in each of my fingers. He dropped his voice, "So what do you think of Tara, Shailu?"

"I think she has the whitest teeth I've ever seen!"

"I think she'll be good company for your Meera Kaku. What with my work and the doctors always telling me to rest, Meera Kaku gets lonely. Tara and she will do the marketing together. She will accompany Meera on her evening rounds of Shivaji Park. Be the daughter we never had! And Tara will have a good home . . ."

"How did her parents die, Kaka?" I asked.

"In a train derailment, Shailu. Tara was only three years old . . . A very dear friend of mine, her father and I were together in school *and* Engineering College. After they died, Tara went to live with her grandmother in Nagpur. When I received news of her grandmother's death, I knew I had to take care of Tara. She has an uncle in Calcutta but doesn't really know him. Arranging for her to come here took a while. I had to get permission from her uncle — and I didn't want to mention anything to anybody until everything was settled. Go and talk to Tara, Shailu. She must be feeling lost."

I climbed down off his lap and went into the kitchen. Tara had just finished rinsing the dishes. She was alone. She smiled at me, picked up a hand towel and started drying the utensils. When that was done she opened drawers and cupboards to see what went where. She didn't seem shy or uncomfortable around Kaku's kitchen. I helped her put everything away.

Afterwards we sat at the kitchen table. Tara carefully re-moved the mogra garland from a long plait, laid it on the table.

She turned me around, secured the garland to a strand of my short hair with a bob pin she pulled out of her own head.

"I bought the garland at Nagpur Station," she said. I removed it from my hair, held it to my nose. I smelled soot, coal. I sniffed once again. Faintly, from somewhere deep within, the sweet scent of mogra rose up to my nostrils. I gave her back the hair pin and held out my hand. She tied the garland around my wrist.

I knew things hadn't improved between Tara and Meera Kaku when about a fortnight after her arrival Kaka asked Mum if she would accompany Tara when she went to register at Ruia College the following week. When Mum said she'd be glad to without asking any questions, Kaka seemed relieved.

Before Tara came to live with them, I went to Kaka and Kaku whenever they called me, maybe two or three times a week. Now I raced across every evening, as soon as my homework was done. Meera Kaku was not curt to me any more, not the way she had been the day Tara arrived. Kaku was a quiet woman and although she didn't ask me many questions, I knew she liked my chatter, for she always listened carefully to everything I said and, unlike Kaka, never forgot the names of my friends or teachers. She sat at her Singer sewing machine whenever she wasn't in her kitchen and sewed clothes for all of us: dresses for me and my cousins, sari blouses and petticoats for her sisters-in-law, cotton shopping bags for the servants.

"Tara is in a big city now!" Kaka said to Kaku, a few days after Tara started going to Ruia College. "She ought to wear five-yard saris like everyone else." The following day, without saying anything to anyone, Meera Kaku went to Matunga and returned with three brand-new saris. I knew that Kaka was very pleased but I could also see that he was careful not to show Kaku his reaction. When he suggested to her that she sew some blouses to match the new saris, Kaku said no, she didn't have the time. Teach Tara then, Kaka urged. "No," Kaku repeated curtly, not looking at him. Although I felt my palms beginning to go wet I was relieved that Tara hadn't returned from college. Outside, the pre-monsoon sun hung fierce in a brassy sky.

When I heard Tara at the door, I removed a brown paper parcel from a cloth bag and handed it to her as soon as she entered the sitting room. She grinned when she saw what was inside: *Aesop's Fables* and a Time-Life book on animals and their habitats.

Soon after Tara started going to Ruia College, Kaka took me into his confidence and told me that he and I had to make sure that Tara knew English well enough to understand her lecturers before the end of term. "Lend her your storybooks, Shaila," he said, "and converse in English whenever you can, at least fifteen minutes every day."

I had great fun helping Tara. I loved playing teacher and even though we giggled a lot, she was a serious student.

One evening, when Tara was struggling to read from my Enid Blyton *Noddy* book, Meera Kaku came out of the kitchen and said, "She'll never learn English that way. That book is too advanced for her. Why don't you lend her your Kindergarten books, Shaila? She needs to start at the beginning." I could see Vinayak Kaka's smile from the corner of my eye.

I ran home, fetched all my Dick and Jane readers. After that, Tara's progress was swift and noticeable.

So now when I handed her the books, she opened *Aesop's Fables* and read aloud "The ant and the dove" and "The bat and the weasel" without making a single mistake. Kaka and I clapped.

"I know Meera fried fresh coconut karanjis earlier this after-noon — I smelled them as soon as I walked in. Go and ask her for some, Shaila. I think this calls for a celebration!"

Kaku must have heard him in the kitchen for she raised her voice and said, "The girl reads two lines and you behave as if she's won a medal! Nobody can have karanji right now. I'm busy!"

When I went home I asked Mum why Meera Kaku was like that with Tara.

"Like what?" Mum asked me.

"Well, sometimes she treats Tara like a servant!"

"Shaila!" Mum's tone warned me that she would not tolerate any disrespect.

"It's just that she's so strict with Tara," I said carefully.

"You know Kaku, Shaila. It takes her forever to like somebody. That's just the way she is. All this was so sudden. Kaka didn't ask Kaku what she thought about Tara coming to live with them. Men think life is so simple. That people become close just because they live under one roof. Now go and wash your hands. Bayabai said dinner was ready almost ten minutes ago."

Late one evening, when the sky was over-filled and pouring with rain, our telephone rang. I was sitting at my desk, finishing my homework. The sudden ringing against the sound of crashing water startled me.

A second later, Mum shouted out for me to remain inside the house. Kaka had suffered a heart attack and she and Dad were going over to help. I rushed to the window, saw them dash across the lane. I took my homework to the hall, sat on the divan.

After what seemed like an hour, the front door opened and Tara walked in. She was wet. I got her a towel from my room and she dried herself, then sat next to me. She looked frightened. I wondered whether she was thinking about her grandmother.

"How is Kaka?" I asked. She shook her head.

"What's going to happen? When is the ambulance coming?"

"It's not coming, Shaila. I phoned and phoned. The lines are down. Couldn't get through to Kaka's heart specialist either. I tried the number so many times —"

"But Dad knows how to treat him, Tara!"

She nodded and said, "Your mother and father are waiting for Mai and Nana to arrive. Only then will they be able to drive to Shah's Dispensary for Kaka's medicine." Mai and Nana, Mum's parents, lived only ten minutes away. Vinayak Kaka was Nana's younger brother.

I gave up trying to do my homework. The clock's ticking was loud and slow.

The front door opened again. This time Mum rushed in. She unhooked her keys from the waist of her sari, hurried to my room. I followed her. She unlocked the safe. The top shelves held Dad's medicines. She searched the labels of several bottles, then picked one up. "It's a substitute, but it'll have to do," she muttered to herself.

When we returned to the hall she turned to Tara, "It took my parents half an hour to get here. Water is knee high everywhere. No way we can get to the Dispensary now . . . Stay with Shaila tonight, Tara."

Tara nodded and pulled an umbrella from the stand but Mum was already hurrying through the door.

As I lay stretched out on the divan that stormy night, my head resting on her lap, listening to the heavy rain pellet our roof in varying frenzy, Tara's warm, dry hands caressed my face and neck, smoothed down the cotton razai that covered my body. Her massage must have lulled me into sleep for I sat up

42

with a start when the doorbell rang. I glanced at the clock. It was one-thirty in the morning. I jumped up, opened the door.

Nana was standing there. He looked bent, old, tired. Dad was behind him, his hand pressed down against the front left side of Nana's chest as if holding his heart in place. Dad looked at Tara. She quickly went forward and helped Nana to the divan; she coaxed him to lie down, and slipped a cushion under his head. I spread the cotton razai over him; it was still warm from my body.

"Good girls," Dad said, drawing us to the far end of the room. "Now listen to me, both of you. I want you to get some sleep. Nana is in shock so I've given him something to calm him down. He'll be resting in no time. Mum won't be back tonight, Shailu, neither will Mai. We're staying with Kaku." He put his arms around Tara and me, hugged us to him. "Don't cry my little Shailu, don't cry. You must be brave. He was a good man. The best I've known." He wiped my eyes with his palms, briefly touched her cheek. "You must be brave too, Tara. All of us are here for you: remember that!" He disappeared into the rain.

Tara and I went to my parents' room and lay down on their bed. I hadn't looked directly at Tara, not once, since Nana had shuffled in. I couldn't bear to see the expression in her eyes. I stared at the ceiling, wide-eyed. The corridor light cast long shadows on the floor. After a while, Tara moved closer, thrust her hand into my smaller one. I squeezed it and looked sideways: her head was bent and her chin was snuggled into her neck. Her body was heaving and her breath was all caught up in chokes. I closed my eyes.

When I opened them again Tara's hand was still in mine. I turned on my side slowly, unwilling to look her in the face. But I needn't have worried because her head was thrown back and

43

her mouth was slightly open. And although her body was curled into a tight knot under the razai, her breathing was even, deep.

I must have fallen asleep again for now Tara was dressed in a white sari dotted with pink feathers. She was standing at Dadar Railway Station, waiting for the Howrah Express to pull in. I clung to her hand. She looked at me and I noticed her teeth were moist and white and she was saying in Kaku's voice "A stitch in time saves nine."

"But there's no hurry to go to Calcutta," I said.

"What can I do?" Tara replied in my voice, clutching *Aesop's Fables* in her hand. "I'm a mouse and not a bird."

Mum was shaking her head at Tara and saying, "You are tall, strong, and graceful."

Dad said, "Books are never judged by their covers."

Tara was leaning out the train window, tying a mogra garland around my wrist. She stroked my head and said in her own voice, "I won't get lost and neither will you because I found out which way the wind was blowing before I made up my mind."

Deafness Comes to Me

Deafness comes to me, takes you away.

I look at my door again and again. The curtain hangs stiff. You do not come.

Ever since the lizard fell on my bed two weeks ago, it is as though, come nightfall, the wall with the wooden door that connects me to the rest of the house becomes a backdrop, a theatrical prop; my room, a stage. Mine is the only name in the list of players for there are no wings, no dramatic entrances, no well-timed exits.

I turn to the window, run my hands up and down iron bars. My fingers stumble on a crack. Even though my nails are short I don't give up. Like black petals falling off a crumbling rose, smooth peels of stripped paint settle softly on the floor.

The crescent moon dangles, a reflective pendant around the neck of a reclining sky. It is the gold chandrakor you gave me so many years ago, twelve days after our son was born, when we both remarked how, on that auspicious night, the full moon dimmed attending stars with its molten radiance. Like your face, you said, running rough thumbs along my smooth edges, undoing the clasp of my new chain, you must shine only for me. Earlier, I had worn a moss green sari with vermilion border. Go and change, you commanded, when you saw me in the hall, two crimson roses in my hair, ready to greet our guests who were coming for the naming ceremony. I smiled to myself. Wore off-white raw silk with tumeric border instead. Even then eyes followed me everywhere that night. But you didn't notice, didn't know that happiness is hard to conceal.

I look up at the doorway. You are not there.

This time it began the night the lizard that makes her home in the terrace garden outside my window lost her footing, fell on my bed. Landed on her back so I could see bleached under-belly, slightly bloated, rubbery, smooth. Zana flicked her off my razai, chased her along the floor. She was halfway up the wall when Zana's bristle broom found her. I quickly lifted the neckline of my gown up to my eyebrows, averted my eyes. Even then I could see the tail squirming and thrashing long after it had been severed from her body. And I knew without being told that my horoscope entered its inauspicious period the very moment that tail lay still.

So I wasn't surprised next morning when I awakened to a frantic bird pecking at my scalp. Large, black wings flapped against my ears, splayed claws gouged my eyes. I couldn't move. The roar of the wings, it was as if my head was trapped inside a drug-crazed dombari's drum.

Next thing I knew, Zana was pinning my hands to my sides, her calm eyes willing mine to take control. After two minutes she must have seen the terror there subside, for she moved away, closed the window above my head.

"That bird attacked me, Zana, that crow was inside my room! You shouldn't have left the terrace door open!"

Zana walked to the door that leads out on the terrace, threw open its double shutters. Arms flailing, she shooed away the crow which I couldn't see, now that my window was shut. She bent over, stepped back in with something in her hands. When she saw I was looking her way she quickly covered whatever it was with the front of her sari.

"Bring it here! Don't *you* start hiding things from me." My voice must have been harsh, on the verge of something I know not what, for she came directly to my bed, held out an object that left a trail on the floor. A nest. Inside, three cracked eggs, albumen oozing out of shallow crevices like polluted water.

"Why did the crow attack me, Zana, why? I didn't do that!"

Zana laid the nest on the windowsill. Stood at the terrace door, small eyes darting, searching the high, collapsible steel awning that hadn't been opened for over six months. Turning to me, she pointed upwards. No doubt broken straws still hung from the spot where the nest must have lodged.

She handed me a comb from my night table then walked towards the door that connects me to the rest of the house, holding the disintegrating nest that had so recently cocooned life.

I looked away from the terrace and that's when I saw you standing in the doorway, yellow curtain flowers nodding in your wake. You moved aside for Zana, walked towards me, your shoulders with the single mole exactly centred between their blades, broad, high colour in your cheeks. You were shaking your head from side to side. But your eyes! They were the gentlest I'd ever seen them. Your lips started to move, then stopped, your mouth slightly open so I could see the two bottom teeth that I know are sharp, the ones that lean inward. You didn't say anything, just ran your fingertips up and down my face, following their trail with your eyes. You were dressed for the office.

When Zana returned, you left.

Deafness comes to me, takes you away.

She brought with her a large basin of water, some cotton wool rolled in brown paper, a small hand towel. She sat beside me and holding my chin steady with one hand, started cleaning my face and neck with the other. She showed me the wet wad of cotton. It was bloodied.

"Her claws," I said. "Why didn't you come sooner, Zana?" She said nothing, continued to clean me until the basin turned pink. She then dried my face. Carefully applied Cibazol to raw stinging cuts.

"The crow wasn't inside the room," Zana moved her lips slowly, thumbs interlocked, fingers flapping. She was shaking her head, pointing at the floor. Zana looks at my eyes when she speaks to me, the only person who does that besides you. She never raises her tone either. I can tell. "The crow wasn't inside," she repeated.

"How do you explain the scratches on my face then?" I said, suddenly complacent. She held my hands in hers, ran the balls of her thumbs along my fingernails. She took a clean slate from under my mattress, started writing: "As soon as I heard your screams I rushed in. You were slapping, scratching your head, face, neck, ears — I thought a bee must have strayed from its hive — Then I saw the crow's shadow on your bed, to-ing and fro-ing across your head. Heard raucous cawing —"

"Are you telling me it was a shadow?" I touched her hand lightly.

She finished writing, handed me the slate. "I'm trying to think how you could have been mistaken." Zana is the only person who tries to explain my actions. Like me, she knows there is always logic in everything I do. Strangeness, maybe, unpredictability, yes, but always logic.

She got off my bed and opened the window she'd previously shut. The sun crept in, still high enough in the sky to crawl through my window that way. This time the shadow on my crumpled bedding was the elongated shadow of iron bars.

She removed a nail cutter from the top drawer of the dressing table. Then slid the cut nails into a small envelope she made with a scrap of paper. While she gathered all her cleaning things together, she was shaking her head from side to side. Just the way you had earlier on. The first time I'd seen either of you do that.

Deafness comes to me, takes you away.

It's a fortnight since that ill-omened lizard fell on my bed. I am too afraid to ask the astrologer how long this period will continue for I fear he will shake his head too.

I keep constant vigil at my doorway. You do not come.

Oh, you come during the day, when Zana is in the room, when Dr. Gupta visits, when Balu is mopping the floors. When our relatives crowd around me, chatter all at once, hold up cloudy slates, make sure that I understand they are doing their best to keep me informed. You may have lost your hearing, their eyes say, but that doesn't mean you should stop living. When Zana sees my fingernails begin to rake my scalp, when I slump back against propped pillows, she suggests everyone go to the dining room where tea is laid out. They quickly get off my bed, rush to the door.

But you never come alone. Never when bright stars nail soft sky with hard, piercing brilliance, when the moon waxes and wanes according to her mood.

"Do not get so agitated!" Dr. Gupta wrote with heavy hand across the chalk board on my wall, on the morning that grief-stricken crow fluttered helplessly outside my window, "Not much was lost when you lost your hearing. Believe me when I say there is nothing left in this world that is worthy of your ears!"

Just as he'd finished writing, you walked in. And I thought

you'd already left for work. Dr. Gupta took you aside, turned his back to me. When I saw your eyes leave his face, rove the walls, I knew right away what the doctor must have said: "Delusions! Why she should be suffering delusions I do not know. I think I will increase the dosage."

No! I wanted to call out to you. Don't listen to him! It is not delusions which make me confused. Just fear. Fear of a universe without sound. Fear of facing a sea of babbling mouths. Fear of losing you.

There is so much I want to say. But you do not come to me, not any more, not the way you used to when our troubles began. Then, my frustration was your frustration, your ache, mine. I held you close as you said — your mouth pressed against my ear for I was only hard of hearing then — "We must get another specialist to examine you. What all the rest are saying is simply not plausible. I've never heard of such a thing happening before! You develop high fever, the doctor prescribes antibiotics and you become —"

"Don't say it!" I said, turning my head swiftly, covering your mouth with mine. I ran my fingertips through your hair. I could feel your exhaustion. I was exhausted too. In less than two minutes you were asleep, warm breath fanning my neck, our ankles tightly intertwined. I felt your body take shape under my palms, your flesh warm, malleable to my touch. I heard you then. Your voice gay, confident, as you held our Dilip for the first time: "I felt it in my bones," you said. "On the day of our engagement, the moment you handed me that sweetened cup of tea: Only *you* would give me a son." Oblivious to Matron who stood in the corner, meticulously folding soft mulmul kerchiefs into tiny triangles. She, who had seen hundreds of women giving birth to hundreds of sons, couldn't help but smile at your words.

The tightness in your voice, possessive, jealous. "I don't want him in my house ever again. I don't care that his wife is your childhood friend. Did you see how he couldn't keep his eyes off you?"

And another: lazy, languorous, expansive, exaggerating. "Your breasts are a deeply quenching two-wave ocean," your mouth reflected moist moonshine, "each wave perfectly capped, gently cresting, one just a little bit higher than the other."

It was that last voice I kept hearing yesterday afternoon, after Zana handed me your message. "I finally got through to Dilip just now," you'd dictated on the phone. "He'll be here in two days. I know his coming will be a tonic for you. I'll see you tomorrow morning. I have a meeting tonight and I don't know how late I'll be."

I twisted the paper in my hands.

It is not my son I need. It is you. I need you.

I must have fallen asleep then for when I woke the room was smaller, the walls squatter, the ceiling loomed like a vault. Purplish-red shadows stretched interminably, the sunshine dropped lustreless to my floor. I turned the fan to full speed. Hotter air swirled around me faster. I began to feel wet. That's when I took off my sari, pulled at the hooks on my blouse, loosened the drawstrings of my petticoat.

I don't know what they told you when you returned home last night. Balu and the cook.

Zana repeated to me what Balu told her. He said he walked into my room with my afternoon tea and found me at the window, "unclothed." (I doubt "unclothed" is what Balu said but that's how Zana put it.) He told her he shouted for the cook who came running, wrapped me carefully in sheets. Zana cried and cried because she wasn't at home when "it" happened. "I had to go to the tailor," she scribbled, "but I could have gone some other time."

I patted her back. "Don't cry! The cook was very gentle, really. She even chose my favourite colour when she brought me a dry sari. Mauve. Look at it, Zana. Do I not look beautiful? Stop crying! Just tell him to come and see me when he comes home. I will not let Dr. Gupta examine me without him."

But Dr. Gupta was waiting outside my room, already too long. He took my pulse, listened to my chest, wrote out a prescription. He kept scratching his arm vigorously, first the left, then the right. Left, right. Then suddenly, he lunged towards the duster that lay alongside my chalk board and rubbed out what he'd written there two weeks ago.

Deafness came to me, took you away.

My wall with its connecting door is an abandoned prop. Curtain flowers lose colour as night enters the dark quarter. I want to tear them down: the curtain, the door, the wall. Want to call out to you. Come to me, come back. I'm sorry for yesterday afternoon. I forgot your note said you would be late coming home. I just wanted you to see me, all of me, that's all. Not only the way I once was but the way I still am. I wanted you to see me. I want you to see.

Awake When All the World Is Asleep

The silk thread that holds together Nalutai Wadkar's string of pearls is fraying yet again, and this time, instead of getting the necklace restrung, she wants to replace it with one that is longer, more sophisticated. When her husband, Bhausaheb Wadkar, tells her about his upward transfer to Vizak, Nalutai sees her opportunity to broach the subject. Not wishing to rush the issue and thereby mitigate her chance for success, she waits a whole week before presenting her case.

"So why bother getting them restrung?" she says to her husband one night, when they're reading in bed. "Why not get a new necklace instead? I'll need more pearls of course, but now that you have a promotion —"

Bhausaheb's glare stops her mid-persuasion. Since he is not barking at her yet, Nalutai quickly changes track and continues, "What if you go ahead to Vizak and I join you later? Veena —"

"Veena has six months before she gets her degree. She can come then," Bhausaheb lowers his book and removes his glasses.

"Malu was saying yesterday . . ."

"I'm listening."

"She's suggesting a boy for Veena and since our daughter's too young to make up her mind about something as important as a husband, I think I should be here to advise her."

"Stay back then. Find her a suitable boy. I don't want to hear how this one's pointed ears twitch like a goat's or how that boy's older brother has a squint and what if Veena's children are cross-eyed replicas of their Kaka —"

"Do you really think I rejected those boys for such . . . such frivolous reasons!"

"Yes, I do," he says, opening his book once again.

Nalutai turns away from her husband. She is so pleased that the second round was won without a fight that she forgets the first was lost. In seamless floating dreams that night, she sells her necklace for twice its value then replaces it with one so rare, so luminous, that the pearls gleam like little moons against her midnight-blue chiffon.

At the breakfast table a few weeks later, Bhausaheb says good-bye to his family. He calls out to Shantabai who is rolling out the chapatis in the kitchen and tells her to fetch him a taxi at ten o'clock because he is catching the noon flight to Vizak. Nalutai tells him there is no need to call a taxi because she has nothing planned for the morning. "The car and driver will take you to the airport," she says.

Just as Bhausaheb is walking out the door, suitcase in hand, the phone rings. It is Malu. She tells Nalutai that the parents of the boy whom she suggested for Veena have arrived by the Rajdhani, that she's meeting them for lunch and would Mrs. W like to join them? Nalutai softly mouths everything her friend is saying to her husband who nods and mouths back, "Yes yes go for your lunch."

As soon as Bhausaheb catches a taxi for the airport, Nalutai telephones her cousin Hema who lives in the boy's hometown and, imparting all the details she has concerning the boy and his family, entrusts Hema with the task of finding out more.

Happy in the knowledge that she has done her bit towards furthering the search for a suitable boy, Nalutai goes for lunch and forms her impressions.

They're a friendly, sociable couple, she notes. I like her China silk — it looks imported. That turquoise colour would really suit Sarla. Maybe I'll invite them for dinner to the Gymkhana tomorrow night. We could stay for Feature Film Friday — which reminds me, I must call Bhosle to remind him to pick up the reels.

She smiles at the boy's parents and is on the verge of extending an invitation when she suddenly decides to wait until after she has heard from Hema.

"They're a well-known, well-respected family," her cousin reports late that night. "He'd make a very good husband from what I gather. There's one thing though . . ."

"Go on!"

"The boy's sister is eccentric. She lives her life by the number five. Wakes exactly at five a.m., vows she will have five children, her entire wardrobe even consists of five shades of the colour red . . . drives her in-laws crazy! You get the picture! Boy's all right though. Hope we hear some good news soon!"

That's what a thorough investigation unearths, Nalutai sighs with relief, applauding her own judgement for deciding to wait before extending the dinner invitation to the Gymkhana. She sits back in bed. Visions of the eccentric sister's dinner plate looking like a neat garden float through her head: vegetables divided into five heaps, chutney into five portions, the rice into an equal number of mounds. I wonder if the wretched girl puts the amti into five containers? No, no, the father-in-law would never tolerate that. Does she eat one mound at a time or does she scoop five together?

Nalutai shudders and even as she is switching off her bed-side lamp, her thoughts curve to her non-identical twins. Sarla is a tall, lithe, fair replica of her mother down to her upright posture and long, shapely toes; Veena has her father's prominent nose, his coarse, wiry hair, strong teeth, stocky build.

Never had to worry about Sarla, Nalutai smiles, recalling fondly the circumstances surrounding Sarla's wedding.

Sarla was only sixteen when Baba Dani's family asked for her hand in marriage. Nalutai said, "No, my daughter is much too young." Three years later, the Wadkars were approached again. Baba now had a PhD in Chemistry, a gold medal which his parents proudly displayed in their sitting room in Nagpur, an excellent job in Bombay. Sarla was entering her final year of college.

Looking at Baba's handsome face and unusual grey-green eyes, Nalutai decided the timing was perfect. She asked for the prospective bridegroom's date and time of birth and was reassured when her trusted astrologer announced that Sarla and Baba's horoscopes matched on every count. The engagement and all the subsequent preparations went exactly as planned until a week before the wedding, when Baba phoned to say that the company flat that was allotted him would not be available for another year. Nalutai panicked. Bhausaheb considered the housing problem temporary, and suggested Baba move in with them for the one-year duration.

After the wedding, Nalutai hovered around the flat, making sure everything was made comfortable for her new son-in-law. One day, he said to her, "Ma, Sarla tells me that you have cancelled all your programs because of me. Would you do that for a son? Think of me as your son, not your son-in-law. Please, phone your friends and tell them you will meet them tomorrow!"

Nalutai was reunited with her rummy group and her Tuesday Bishi group. She started going to the Gymkhana and resumed charge of Feature Film Fridays. She began organizing dances for youngsters who twisted to Tom Jones and the Beatles, managed Tombola, presided over Bingo. She was welcomed back by Gymkhana members who fondly call her Watertight Wadkar for her ability to keep confidences to herself.

When Baba comes home in the evening, he often finds Sarla practising yoga on a cane chatai in their bedroom. Sometimes he lifts his wife by her legs as she does her headstands, carries her upside down to the bed. Looking at her flushed face, the deep, rhythmic movement of her chest, he lowers his head and muffles her protests with his mouth. They keep their movements swift, to the point, for the door is never locked and in their minds the possibility of someone walking in lends their activity a furtiveness that makes it all the more pleasurable.

A couple of weeks after Bhausaheb has left for Vizak, there is a knock on the bedroom door. Sarla is standing on her head; Baba is contemplating action. "Come in!" he calls out.

Veena pushes open the door and puts her head around it.

"I've almost finished," Sarla tells her.

"I want to show this to Baba," Veena says.

She is holding up her economics textbook. "I was reading today's newspaper. There's an interesting article . . . ," she says.

"Why don't you go to the sitting room, Baba?" Sarla suggests. "That way Veena and you can discuss to your hearts' content. In fact, maybe that's what you should do. Have your tea with Veena every evening, debate your boring theories . . ."

"You look tired Saru, are you all right?" Veena asks.

"I'm fine. Go on now. I still have to take a bath." Sarla enters the bathroom.

Baba and Veena start having their afternoon tea together. Every chapter in Veena's book is examined, argued over, analyzed. Veena is delighted that she can talk to someone about her beloved economics. She misses her father and the discussions they used to have.

Sarla is pleased that she can finish her yoga in peace. Lately, her stomach rumbles hollow even after a sumptuous meal, her breasts feel increasingly tender to the touch and she sees blue veins in them she didn't notice before. She wants to be left alone.

The explanation creeps up on her, right in the middle of a lecture on polygamy in the tribal communities of Assam.

She rushes home and finds Veena in the kitchen, helping Shantabai shell peas. She pulls Veena to her room.

"What? Quickly!" Veena laughs.

Sarla tells her.

"Me! An aunt! This is happening sooner than I thought."

"You can say that again!"

"Are you sure? How do you feel? Can I get you something?"

"Oh Veena, you're too good to be true! I believe you're as excited as I am. If only you get married now, everything will be perfect!"

"I'll make a better aunt than a wife, Saru."

"Don't say that!"

"You know what I mean. I must finish college, then a Master's and then who knows, an interesting job somewhere, maybe even a PhD."

"Baba thinks you have every potential of becoming a Nobel laureate!" Sarla has confidence in her husband's judgement.

"Won't your son be proud of me then!"

"Don't leave it for too long." Sarla is serious.

"What?"

"Marriage, Veena. Then we'll have more to share."

"Don't you start! Besides, the Ruminating Unquenchable Moonstruck Myopic Yammering Rummy Group are bound to come up with the perfect match sooner or later . . ."

They giggle together.

After that day, Sarla stops doing yoga. She feels lethargic, listless. She begins to sit in on Veena's and Baba's discussions but soon gives that up: the smell of tea enters her gut like a malodorous vapour and she has to rush to the bathroom every time. Nothing seems to please her.

One day, Nalutai says, "You need a change, Sarla. Why don't you start coming with me in the evenings? It'll take your mind off your discomfort."

Veena rolls her eyes in Sarla's direction. They both know how Really Utopic Magically Meaningfully Ya-hoo the Rummy Group can be!

"I don't think so, Ma," Sarla says. "The doctor told me it'll soon be over. She said it's only in the first trimester."

"You need to get your mind diverted, Sarla."

Sarla decides to accompany her mother for a few days after which she will plead tiredness. Leave it to Ma's groups, she has to admit a fortnight later, to take action and come up with a solution. Between them they find a pregnant daughter-in-law and bring her to their evenings.

Kumud and Sarla sit in one corner and exchange notes while ignoring everyone else. They eat huge quantities of whatever the hostess has prepared and Sarla is so glad for the temporary diversion that she does not mind the endless cups of tea Kumud gulps in attempts to quench her bottomless thirst.

⌒

Shantabai stands at the kitchen window, looking down at the Maya Building playground. The surrounding lawn is a dull green under blocks of dark evening shadow. The air feels laden, clammy, the atmosphere is oppressive, dense. Suddenly impatient for a breath of fresh air, Shantabai quickly serves Baba and Veena their tea, then goes downstairs to the playground where the daily assembly is already in session: every evening, a congregation of cooks, ayahs, and servants compare households, exchange gossip, air grievances, while keeping an eye on the children of the families they serve. Sometimes, Shantabai contributes bits and pieces to the conversation but never says anything directly critical of "her family."

This particular day, however, she is upset. Nalutai has informed Shantabai that she will be required to go to her friend Malu's house the end of the following month because Malu's cook is going away on leave. Every year Malu's cook takes a month off and Nalutai sends Shantabai as a replacement.

"Their kitchen is filthy!" Shantabai complains to Hiru, a calm-eyed man who looks after Chaganlal Saheb's three boys on the fifth floor. "Every time I go there I must scrub and scrub for one hour before kitchen is fit to boil water for cup of tea!"

"Same thing you are complaining about every year, Shantabai!"

"What to do! Last time I found rat-droppings on backs of shelves . . . hundreds of cockroaches must I not have killed? Nalutai has never entered Mrs. Malu's kitchen or she'd never ask me to go there . . ."

"Tell her once and for all that you are not wanting to go as replacement," Hiru advises.

Shantabai turns her head and watches the children on the merry-go-round.

"You are not telling Nalutai because it is not being any use!

60

We were born to serve, you and I . . . nobody can change that . . . ," Hiru begins.

Shantabai smiles at him, nods her head in agreement for she knows she cannot refute that which she is about to hear. Hiru's simple, unchanging philosophy is well known to the daily assembly.

". . . so whyfor grumble? Who can change Fate? It is watching over all of us . . . It is awake when all the world is asleep."

The next day, on a particularly quiet, motionless evening, Baba and Veena sit in the living room, sipping minted tea. When Veena bends over, pouring Baba's second cup, the mogra garland she is wearing in her hair slips and falls into his cup. Baba leans across, plucks it out of the tea, and after removing his handkerchief from his pocket, gently mops the petals. The ones that are beginning to go transparent he discards. He takes Veena by her shoulders, turns her around, removes a pin from her hair and secures the garland back in its place. It isn't until his fingers touch her warm neck that Veena moves away, blushing. She rushes to the opposite side of the room, gulps her cooling tea and hurriedly leaves the room.

That night at the dinner table, Veena says, "Ma, I'm getting bored at home without Saru. Can't I come with you?"

"I don't think so, Veena. Or soon all the daughters and daughters-in-law will be asking to come."

"Please, Ma . . . I don't want to stay behind when you two are having such a good time. What do you think, Saru?"

"I think Ma is right, Veena," Sarla is apologetic; she hates to agree with Ma if it means disagreeing with Veena. But she is reluctant to include her sister in the increasingly intimate chats she and Kumud are having. Who else can she tell about the indifference she experiences when Baba comes near her, the reluctance with which she sometimes gives in to him, the remoteness she feels from people who do not share her condition, the wonder and trepidation with which she views the germinating life within her?

"I have a better idea, Veena. If you're getting bored at home why not go to the Gymkhana for a swim?" Sarla suggests.

"That's a good idea," Baba says.

From that day forward, instead of coming home for afternoon tea, Veena goes to the Gymkhana. She loses count of the number of laps completed as she finishes lengths and breadths, blots her mind of all thoughts except the latest chapter in economics.

One evening she arrives at the pool to find it closed for repairs. She kneels at the edge of the water, mesmerized by the pool lights spiralling downwards. A low buzz, a whirring, humming sound fills her ears. She shifts her gaze. Metallic bluebottles, bloated bumblebees, graceful dragonflies, giddily collide into each other as they fight for a place in front of the warm lights.

Baba is the light and I am the giddy one — the admission slices through her. She touches the mogra garland in her hair, caresses her neck. She sits back on her haunches and wraps her arms around her knees. The ghost of a breeze coming off the water is cold.

A week later, after Baba has left for work and the girls for college, Shantabai asks Nalutai, "Have you found anyone for Veena yet?"

Shantabai has been with the family since the birth of the twins and assumes certain — the girls would say well-deserved — rights when it comes to them. Nalutai normally tolerates this liberty but today she resents the interference; she has been too busy to check out yet another boy, this time suggested by Bhausaheb's sister.

"No, not yet."

"What problem is, I don't understand," Shantabai wonders. "Our Veena is one in a lakh! Ideal wife will she not make?"

"Yes, yes. But why are you bringing this up now? The maalishwali will soon be here for my massage."

"I saw them yesterday."

"Saw who?"

"Baba Saheb and Veena!"

"Have you lost your head?"

"They were holding hands."

"Who?"

"Baba Saheb and —"

"Don't talk nonsense. When?"

"I am downstairs, sitting on compound wall . . ."

"Yes, yes."

"Not sure stove is turned off under pressure cooker so I come up and . . ."

"Go on Bai!"

"think I'll clear tea things from sitting room and I see them."

"What did they say?"

"Say?"

"Yes, Shantabai! What did they say when they saw you? Are you deaf?"

"They don't see me. They're looking out of window . . . I don't go in, just stand in doorway, leave flat, go downstairs."

"There must be an explanation. Holding hands did you say? Were you wearing your glasses?"

"I am only needing them for reading!"

"Remember what Dr. Bhandare said when I took you for a checkup last time? He said you were developing a cataract in one eye. Standing by the window did you say — that means you were looking into the light . . ."

"I saw what I saw."

"There must be an explanation. Don't tell anyone, do you hear? I want no gossip amongst the Maya Building servants and cooks! I'll talk to Veena before I leave for Vizak. Or maybe on my return — no, it better be before although I don't know when. There's the doorbell — must be the maalishwali. Go on! Answer it! And don't worry so much — there must be an explanation."

Shantabai is aware Nalutai has a lot to do before she leaves for Vizak. She is hosting the rummy group in a few days' time and the final menu is still to be decided. The election for the Gymkhana's new board of executives is around the corner. Nalutai wants to retain her position as social secretary but the competition is keen and she has yet to garner the necessary support.

Since it will be a while before Nalutai will find time to talk to Veena, Shantabai decides to take matters into her own hands: she stops her evening outings to the playground. She bangs pots and pans as she goes about her cooking, roams the rooms with duster and mop, polishes already shining doorknobs, asks for Veena's help in the kitchen.

I must have been mistaken, Shantabai reassures herself, a few days later. They even sit on opposite sides of room and Veena is always willing to help me . . .

Shantabai decides there is no need to pester Nalutai to talk to Veena before leaving for Vizak.

The morning before Nalutai is to leave, Sarla wakes up Baba. There is blood on her sheet. He wakens Ma.

The doctor examines Sarla and says a little spotting is perfectly normal.

"I'm leaving for Vizak for a few days tomorrow. Can I take Sarla with me?" Nalutai asks the doctor.

"There's no need, Ma . . ."

"It doesn't matter either way. Just don't overdo things, Sarla. There's not much else I can suggest," the doctor says.

"I won't be so worried if Sarla is with me, Doctor. It's too late to cancel my going now. It's better you come with me, Sarla."

Nalutai doesn't waste time trying to book her ticket through the airline office. Instead, she rings her brother-in-law who is an MLA — a member of the legislative assembly.

"What is it? I'm on my way to a meeting!" he says.

"I need an airline ticket, Bhauji. You see —"

"For when?"

"Tomorrow afternoon. I'm —"

"I'm not travelling anywhere tomorrow. Assembly is in session. Speak to my secretary."

He puts down the phone. Nalutai dials his number again and this time speaks to his secretary. There's a quota set aside for MLAs needing to travel on urgent business; the secretary says he'll see what he can do.

He calls her back. "The plane is completely booked but I did manage to find you a ticket — the last one. I'll send it with the peon this evening." He disconnects the phone.

"They're always in such a hurry to bang the phone down!" Nalutai grumbles to Sarla.

Her daughter smiles. "I'm sure they have better things to do at the legislative offices, Ma, than to organize last-minute air tickets for pregnant nieces!"

Nalutai cancels her programs for the evening and stays with Sarla. Veena misses her last lecture and comes home early. When she hears that Sarla is accompanying Ma the next day, she says, "I want to come as well."

"You should have asked for two tickets, Ma," Sarla says.

"It wouldn't have done any good, we were lucky to get the last one."

"I'm coming with you."

"Don't be difficult, Veena," Ma says.

"Stay here Saru, I'll look after you," Veena turns to her sister.

"What is it, Veena?" Sarla asks.

"You don't need to take her with you, Ma. Shantabai and I are here," Veena says.

"And don't forget Baba!" Sarla smiles.

"How can you joke, Sarla? This is a matter of life and death — your baby, think of that."

"Don't be ridiculous, Ma. You're always exaggerating! I heard what the doctor said."

"I go to all that trouble to get you this ticket and what do you want me to do? Call Bhauji and cancel it? Have the phone slammed down on me again?"

"You got the ticket not for Saru but because you didn't want to worry about her when you were away," Veena says. "And did you ask me whether I wanted to come or did it never occur to you that I might be missing Papa too?"

"This is ridiculous, Veena, and why are you crying? For God's sake, what has gotten into you?" Her conversation with Shantabai, about Veena and Baba, flashes into Nalutai's mind. She raises her eyebrows at Shantabai who is standing in the corner. Shantabai shakes her head as if to indicate that she does not know what Veena's outburst is about. Maybe it's that time of the month for Veena, Nalutai thinks.

"What's gotten into me? Why am I crying? I'm crying because I'm upset, Ma! That's why people cry. God! When will you start seeing things!"

"It's only a fortnight, Veena! I'll be back soon," Sarla says, wondering whether her sister has been overworking for the BA finals. She looks inquiringly at Veena.

But Veena only says, "Not soon enough Saru . . . Don't go!"

"It's just as well Baba isn't here or what would he think of all this fuss over nothing?" Ma says.

"That's all you're concerned about. What others think. Not what I or Saru or Papa . . . Did you ever stop and think what people really think about you? About your not joining Papa so that you can play your rummy, organize your precious films at the Gymkhana . . ."

Shantabai comes and puts her arms around Veena's shoulders. "Don't get so upset Veena, I'll be here and before you know, Sarla will be back."

"You calm her down Shantabai — she won't listen to anything I say. And oh yes, before I forget, Malu's cook left this morning —"

"But you said . . ." Shantabai drops her arms from Veena's shoulders.

"I know, I know, she was supposed to go next month, but she told Malu that her mother was taken ill — a concocted story without doubt — so she needed to go early. I promised Malu that you would go there between five and eight every evening. Her driver will pick you up and bring you back in time for Baba Saheb's and Veena's dinner."

"But that's not possible. It's the time I cook evening meal —"

"Don't say another word, Shantabai! I promised Malu over a month ago. And make sure you don't prepare anything special for them — we'll reserve those dishes for when they dine with us! . . . Do some yoga, Veena, it'll calm you down."

Shantabai is shaking her head from side to side when Veena runs out of the room.

That night Sarla tells Baba about that afternoon.

67

"That's why Veena looked tearful all through dinner! Tell you what . . . we'll go early to the airport and see if there are any last-minute cancellations. She should go with you to Vizak," Baba says.

"Should go with us?" Sarla asks him. "Why?"

"You said she's missing Papa, didn't you? And you think she's studying too hard? I meant it'll be a good break for her, that's all."

Veena is optimistic on the way to the airport.

"Now don't build up your hopes too much, Veena," Nalutai cautions. "It's always bedlam at the cancellations desk."

"Yes Ma, yes."

Not only is there bedlam but Baba can't even see the person who is handling the cancellations, only a cluster of bodies which appears to be converging.

"Give Ma a hug, go on!" Sarla whispers in Veena's ear as Ma is about to enter the departure lounge.

After giving Ma a hug, Veena walks out of the airport. Baba joins her in the car. They go home in silence.

Shantabai has prepared Veena's favourite vegetable — deep-fried ladies fingers stuffed with fresh, spicy coconut. Veena tries to give the impression of enjoying her dinner but every mouthful goes dry as it approaches her throat.

That night she lies on her back and, like all the nights since her mogra garland fell into Baba's teacup and his warm fingers brushed her neck, she relaxes her body and repeats to herself:

"My mind is a still serene pool beneath a blue breezeless sky. My thoughts my feelings, sharp-edged shards that shatter its calm surface then spread and spread in concentric circles. I will summon these thoughts, gather these feelings, hurl them from my consciousness to a place where the sun does not rise, the moon does not glow. I will chant Om until there are no

68

thoughts no feelings no pool no blue only Om which is Everything and Nothing. Om . . . mmm . . . mmm."

But when Baba touches her the next day there is no room
for pledges, only sensation and exhilaration and longing, and
a deep deep ache because everything is so wrong yet feels
so good.

Baba and Veena fetch Sarla and Ma from the airport.

When they come home, Veena follows Sarla into her room.
Baba, Veena, and Sarla sit on the bed as Sarla gives them news
of Papa. When she is finished, she gets up to use the bathroom.
As she is walking away, Sarla sees a movement out of the corner
of her eye; she spins around. Veena is snatching her hand away
from Baba's.

She looks into Veena's face and screams, "MA!"

Nalutai and Shantabai come running.

Standing in the doorway, Shantabai covers her mouth with
the end of her sari. She hadn't expected Sarla to find out so
quickly. She looks at Baba. He is at the window, peering out
into the street. She wonders whether he is thinking what she's
thinking: that none of this would have happened if the company flat had been ready on time.

Sarla tells her mother what she believes to be the truth and
says: "It's all your fault, Ma. Short of prostrating herself Veena
begged you to let her come with us. I should not have gone to
Vizak . . . Nothing was wrong with me. But you don't listen, do
you? Once you get something into your head, that's it, nothing
else matters . . . Everything is beginning to make sense now!
You knew, Veena, didn't you," Sarla continues, turning to Veena
who is still sitting on the bed, her eyes shut tight, "that something like this would happen? . . . That's why you were so upset
when you heard I was going with Ma!"

Sarla stands over her mother who is slumped in the armchair next to the bed and pokes her in the arm. "You still don't see Ma, do you? If only you'd listened to Veena, I would not have gone with you and none of this would have happened."

But all Ma is thinking is how she should not have sent Shantabai as a substitute cook to Malu's.

Sarla is saying: "As for you Veena . . . Our Vigorous Supple Twosome is now the Venomous Slain Twosome! What a joke! Volte-Face Veena. Vicious Venal Veena. Ha! I have it! Vampish Veena and Besotted Baba. Bumbling Base Bubonic Baba!"

Veena, who has opened her eyes, cannot bear the mad look on Sarla's livid face, cannot bear her hysterical name-game. She covers her ears with a pillow and shuts her eyes in the vain hope of obliterating the sign that is etching itself into *her* head: Pool — Closed for Repairs.

Nalutai stands over her and screams, "Is this true, Veena? Is this true? You shameless girl, what did I do to deserve this?" She drags Veena off the bed and pulls her to the sitting room where she slaps her face repeatedly, willing her to deny the accusation, say something, anything. Baba intervenes, standing between them.

"Get out of my house right now. Right now. Out!" Ma shouts at Veena. Wanting to inflict pain on this foolish, ungrateful girl, she catches Veena by her hair, drags her to the front door.

Baba pleads, "It's all my fault, Ma. Veena is innocent. It's all my fault. Don't blame her."

"Innocent! She's leaving my house tonight."

"Don't do that! You throw her out of this house and I will be forced to look after her."

Can't let Sarla's life be wasted, Nalutai is frantic, I must protect Sarla. She looks at Veena who is leaning against the

70

front door. I should have married her to the boy with the wretched sister so mesmerized by the number five —

"Listen to me, Ma!" Baba is saying. "Try and understand what I'm suggesting: I will find a suitable boy for Veena. I'll convince her that ours was just an infatuation, that I have Sarla and the baby. Don't blame Veena. She did not know what she was doing. It's all my fault. I'll write Papa a letter tonight, explain what has happened, ask him what we should do. But please, don't turn her out. You do that and I will be forced to look after her! Don't throw her out!"

Nalutai hisses at Baba, "And what do you think Papa is going to suggest? You fool. Nobody is going to be forced to look after her. Least of all you — you'll stay here with your wife!"

Sarla comes out of her room, looks down the corridor. She sees Ma who continues to be deaf, sees the once-vital Veena, now stooping, demolished, sees Baba who will not speak to her, will not meet her eyes.

Veena looks at Sarla and taking the end of her sari, throws it over her own head. Shantabai brings Veena's chappals and puts them on her feet. Veena reaches down, takes them off, slaps them on top of her covered head. Shantabai snatches the chappals and puts them back on Veena's feet. "Never do that. It'll bring you Pauper's Luck!" she admonishes and puts her arms around the girl.

Still not looking at Sarla, Baba puts on his shoes. "Where do you think you're going!" Nalutai is screaming at him. "Don't you dare leave this house!"

Baba takes his mother-in-law by her shoulders and walks her backwards, towards his wife.

Shantabai gently takes the pallu off Veena's head.

Veena looks at Sarla. They all do. They see her dishevelled look, loosened hair brushing blotched face, red eyes dark and swollen. Only Veena sees in that twin-face so much pity and sorrow and regret that she hasn't the courage to utter a single word. She stumbles out the front door and it is not until she is outside the Maya Building that she acknowledges the conviction that was so clearly chiselled into her sister's face: We twins are never going to see each other again.

A Miracle

Saroj Atya opens her eyes. A blurred silhouette stands outlined against the windowscape. The sky is dyed pink and gold by the rising sun. A nasal, muffled voice is saying, "Hand over your flat to Gaja today! Go live in Bicholim. Do this and I, Vithoba, will make your heart His house forever!" Saroj Atya gropes for her glasses, adjusts them on her nose. A glimpse of the disappearing sole of his right foot as he runs away, sixth digit forking out from the base of his big toe like a bulbous cactus, sets Atya's loose, crumpled body jiggling with laughter.

"You should have worn chappals, Gaja!" she laughs. "You spoiled the trick, son." Atya removes her glasses, pats her eyes with the end of her sari. "Muli! Muli? Where are you, girl?" she calls out. "Did you let Gaja in?" Muli doesn't answer.

"Hmmm!" Atya breathes out, glancing across the room at her husband, Bapusaheb, who lies on his back, chest heaving rhythmically, mind dormant. The front door bangs shut.

Still dizzy from sitting up too quickly, Saroj Atya clutches the edge of her mattress, pulls herself to her feet. On top of her bedside dresser stands a six-inch silver statue of her favourite deity, Vithoba. Bending over and touching her forehead to the single marigold at His feet, she says, "Thank-you, Vithoba, thank-you. It is all because of You that our adopted son is back.

73

Now only one thing remains. You know how my heart craves for that moment when Bapusaheb will sit up in bed, restored. Grant me this and I will be emptied of all worldly desires. I will be ready to die."

Atya crosses the room, stands over Bapusaheb. She scans his body carefully while all the time willing it to respond. But this morning there is nothing, not even the slightest flutter. When it comes to praying and fasting for Bapusaheb's recovery it matters not the least what the doctors have repeatedly told her: that his twitches are involuntary, his coma irreversible.

"Muli! Kuthay ahais ge? Pay her to be my right hand but is she there when I need her?" Atya mutters, lumbering down the corridor towards the kitchen.

The bathroom door opens. An herb-like, moist fragrance precedes Muli as she saunters out. Her eyes widen when she sees Atya. She grasps the sodden towel draped around her lower half, pulls it up to cover sturdy breasts. "What you doing up so early, Atya Bai? It is not being five-thirty yet!" Muli gasps.

"Did you see Gaja? Get some clothes on, girl! Is this how you prance around in the mornings? Did you let him in?"

"Gaja Dada? Not me!" Muli runs past Atya into the spare bedroom. She removes the wet towel from around her body, throws it over the drying wire. The explanation of how Gaja must have entered the flat catches her unawares. Oh no, she mutters to herself, hastily tying the drawstring of her petticoat, I am forgetting to bolt door when I am coming back into flat middle of night. Gaja, the badmaash, must have used his latch-key. It is just as well Atya is not knowing about my hours on landing with Laxmandriver or else it will be chutti for me. Muli giggles; visions of Laxmandriver's foresty moustache exploring bare skin make her body tingle. But doubt enters her mind. She raises her voice, "Gaja Dada here? At this hour? Not possible,

Atya Bai! Give me minute and I am making you nice, hot tea."

Saroj Atya is sipping her second sweetened cup when she hears Muli walking down the corridor. She quickly hides the sugar caddy under a hand towel. No doctor-shoctor is going to keep her from eating what she wants today! When Muli enters the kitchen, Atya has already planned her feast for the Return of Gaja. "We'll make sweet semolina shira, eggplant bharit in lots of curds, and fried pomfret. Be first at the fish market this morning, Muli: choose the pomfret with the clearest eyes!" she says.

Muli shakes her head. "Don't be disappointed when Gaja Dada is not coming. You were dreaming. And if he was here, why was he not staying?"

"Who knows why Gaja does or doesn't do something! But I tell you Muli, he's in good spirits this time. When was the last time he played a trick on me . . .? I remember. It was when he came to our door dressed like a beggar, eyelids turned inside out, one leg folded back to look like a stump — What a disguise! I didn't recognize him until all the food in his bowl was eaten and he'd grinned at me. But I knew it was him this morning, Muli. Who else has eleven toes? Not our Lord Vithoba. Only my Gaja!" Atya laughs, wiping her eyes with the end of her sari.

Muli doesn't know anything about Gaja's tricks because that was before her time, before she came to work for Bapusaheb and Saroj Atya. What she does remember is Gaja's last visit home, when he had crooked a finger at her, eyes beckoning, a supplicating smile on his face. She had tossed her head, growled under her breath, let him know she didn't feel threatened, not in the least. Nevertheless, just to make sure Gaja would stay in line, she complained about him to Laxmandriver the following morning, whereupon Laxmandriver, in his characteristic yet chivalrous fashion, took care of the matter instantly. That evening, he cornered Gaja in the parking lot and, flexing his moustache to villainous effect, threatened to cut off Gaja's cucumber if Gaja even as much as glanced in Muli's direction again. The story then spread, with lewd laughter and much thigh-slapping, amongst the drivers of Maya Building: how Gaja had slunk away, his armpits patchy with sweat, his hair standing erect, now the only part of his anatomy capable of being stiff.

Muli sighs: that was almost a year ago. She carries Saroj Atya's teacup to the basin. "Don't tell me I am not warning you, Atya Bai, when you are pacing flat tonight, gas pains shooting darts into your heart!" she says.

Atya is not surprised by Muli's precise description of flatulence brought on by disappointment, for hasn't Muli seen Atya — and stood by her — throughout Bapusaheb's illness? "All right! So you've warned me. Now run water for my bath," Atya says, reaching for a glucose biscuit.

Muli turns on the hot water tap in the bathroom, cranks the handle of the geyser. While the bucket is being filled she opens the top drawer of Atya's dresser. After removing a bottle of Hajmola Churan, she briefly glances at the illustration on its label. A relieved face, cloudy puff of air escaping grinning mouth, assures her that she has the right medication for Atya's impending indigestion. She takes it to the dining room, places it on the centre of the table.

Gaja comes in the evening, drawn by the heady aromas that emanate from Saroj Atya's kitchen, fragrant spices that twist the gut of his memory, pull him homeward. He lets Atya embrace him, breathes in her briny perspiration mingled with Mysore Sandalwood Soap.

76

There is a calm, satiating peace at the dinner table as Gaja and Atya squeeze fresh lime juice down the length of fried pomfrets, remove their delicate, white bones with care. They lick salty yoghurt off their fingers, consume vast quantities of semolina shira studded with cardamoms and saffron.

When Muli silently refills Gaja's empty plate, he doesn't as much as glance at her.

After dinner, Saroj Atya takes Gaja in to see Bapusaheb.

If only Bapusaheb were well enough to see you today, she thinks. You resemble my brother so much. The same slightly elongated shape of head, curly hair lying low on neck, eyes all but disappearing when you smile . . .

Gaja is staring at Bapusaheb. The hopelessness of the vacant, still face, oxygen and feeding tubes running out of nose and mouth hooks into his sensibility, but only for a moment. He is here for a purpose, he reminds himself, switching off the light before leaving the room.

He takes a handful of raw cashew nuts from a glass jar in the kitchen and sits on the swing on the front verandah. Atya leans against a bolster on the divan opposite. She says, "Thought you would play a trick on old Atya this morning, did you? Can't fool me, boy! What did you think you were doing, pretending to be Vithoba? And what was that you were saying? About Bicholim?"

Gaja swallows a mouthful. "What do you mean?"

Atya chuckles, wagging a finger at him.

"I just got in from Poona. By the Deccan Queen. Look!" he says. "Let me show you my train ticket!" He empties his pockets, brings up loose change, a knotted handkerchief, a latchkey to Atya's flat. No ticket.

"You were in Poona? With Chotu?" Saroj Atya asks.

"No, no, not Chotu — I'm tired, Atya. That train must have

made a thousand unscheduled stops. I think I'll go to bed."
Gaja yawns.

"All right, all right. So you don't want to admit it was
you dressed up as Vithoba! Go to sleep, you look exhausted.
Your night clothes, everything in your wardrobe is just the
way you left it," Atya smiles. "Ask Muli if you need anything
else."

Gaja stops the swing with his feet, straightens his torso.
"It feels so good to be back I think I'm going to stay forever,"
he says.

Atya stretches out on the divan, folds her arms under her
head. Her gaze is drawn towards Venus. She thinks she has
found the North Star.

Gaja is shaking Saroj Atya. "Wake up! Why are you sleeping
out on the verandah? Listen to what happened!"

Atya sits up slowly. The thick razai Muli must have laid over
her is damp with dew; Atya throws it off. The early-morning air
clings moist and sultry.

Muli comes to the verandah, sets down a tray. Atya swallows
the bitterness that has collected in her mouth with a gulp of tea.

"Vithoba came to me last night!" Gaja is excited.

"He appeared in your dreams?"

"Not in my dreams, in person!"

"Just the way He appeared to me yesterday morning," Atya
smiles.

"I know nothing about that," he says. "Vithoba told me
this flat belongs to me!"

"I'm not surprised, Gaja. The whole world knows the flat is
to be yours after us. Why wouldn't He?"

"Don't make fun of me. I want you to leave — right now,
today!"

"Today? That's not in our hands, Gaja, but the time will come sooner than you think."

"I don't mean *then*, I mean right now." Muli comes out on the verandah. Gaja is shouting.

"Where will we go?" Atya says.

"Bicholim. The rest of your family is there."

"But you are our family!"

"Don't get sentimental, Atya. I mean it. I want the flat. Now!"

"Don't be foolish, boy! You can stay here, with us. This flat belongs to all —"

"I want it now or else . . ."

"Or else what, Gaja?"

"I will make life miserable for you."

"Well, go ahead and do that, son!" Atya says, standing up, nodding at Muli to remove the tray.

Gaja starts treating the flat like a hotel, comes and goes whenever he pleases; when he orders Muli to serve him food at odd times of the day, Muli is stoic. This time she and Atya are allies. She serves Atya her meals in the kitchen when Gaja takes over the dining table, litters it with books, newspapers, cigarettes, pencils. He tells Atya he is working on a draft to present to the courts. He says he is going to sue for the flat. In front of Gaja, Atya maintains a yogic calm.

But whenever a windstorm rages, thrashing her innards with a whip-like fury, racking her torso with pain, Atya consoles herself: Every day that passes is one day less towards that day when Gaja will get fed up and leave. And when he does, Vithoba, I promise You: I will renounce my worldly goods. But until then, I will not give in!

Late one evening, after pacing the verandah two hundred times, Atya walks into the kitchen to see Muli deftly avoiding

Gaja's embrace. That night she takes Muli to sleep with her in her bedroom and bolts the door.

Gaja is quarrelsome, irritable the next day. Atya and Muli are determined to be patient. They can sense the end drawing near. Frustrated by their quiet indifference, he leaves the flat after dinner.

"I heard you all day, Atya Bai, talking to Bapusaheb," Muli says. "What good is that?"

Saroj Atya shakes her head. "The boy has lost his reason, Muli. I don't know what to do!"

"Talk to Janaki Bai. She asked how you were when she saw me on landing this morning. Go on, I'll keep eye on Bapusaheb," Muli says.

Atya goes to the Joshis' across the landing. Arjun, their twenty-five-year-old son, opens the door.

"Come in Atya, come in! I heard Gaja shouting at you this morning. I wanted to knock his teeth out. See this fist? Just give me the word!" Arjun says.

Atya takes his fist, unfurls the tightly gripped fingers. "It's not fists we need, Arjun . . . When I should have bent the rod, I didn't. I'm afraid it's too late now!"

"Never too late, Atya. That good for nothing doesn't deserve you or Bapusaheb. But come in and sit down. We've just finished dinner."

Arjun leads Saroj Atya into the sitting room where his parents, Vinod and Janaki, and twin brother, Arun, are gathered around the coffee table. Vinod is dealing out from a pack of cards. When Janaki sees Atya she quickly stands up and asks her to take a seat on the sofa.

"I'll come another time. Didn't mean to disturb your rummy," Atya says.

"No, no, please, take a seat. You're not disturbing anything.

How are things with Gaja?" Janaki's voice is sympathetic.

Atya sighs. "He's obsessed I tell you! Determined to throw us out of the flat. Wants it all for himself. And to think I was so happy to see him," she says, covering her right shoulder with the end of her sari.

"I don't understand this wanting the flat business. Why can't all three of you live together?" Janaki asks.

Saroj Atya shakes her head. "I don't know. That first morning — when Gaja came back — I thought he was playing a trick on me, pretending to be Vithoba, telling me to go live in Bicholim. But now he is insisting Lord Vithoba appeared to him. In person, if you please. Seems Vithoba told him the flat belongs only to him."

"I bet you anything Gaja is desperate," Arjun says. "Pretending to be Vithoba was probably his last resort to get you to leave, Atya. He knows the flat cannot be his while you or Bapusaheb are alive!"

"But what is he going to do with the flat?" Saroj Atya looks around the room.

"Sell it," Arun says. "Do you know the black market price for flats like ours is in the several lakhs?"

Atya turns to Janaki. "I should have listened to Bapusaheb when he warned me not to spoil Gaja. 'Soon Gaja'll have you eating off his feet,' he'd say."

"Do we not all of us spoil our children?" Janaki rubs her palm up and down Atya's back. "Don't blame yourself, Saroj! I remember Gaja when he was small — such a sweet boy. Always smiling. Took good care of you, too . . . 'Blood pressure, Atya! No climbing stairs!' he'd wag a little finger when you were too impatient to wait for the lift. Such a sweet boy."

Atya smiles. "I remember. I didn't dream then that one day he would turn out to be just like my brother. Bapusaheb and I thought we'd gotten rid of that possibility when we adopted him. But now I can't help thinking: like my brother who abandoned his family, will Gaja one day leave us too? Leave us to wonder forever whether he is dead or alive?"

"Bas, Saroj, bas," Janaki says. "Don't think about all that. We'll find a way out of this. Here, drink this water."

Atya takes the glass. They all sit in silence as she drains it. Janaki looks at Arjun.

"Not to worry, Atya. I'll speak to Gaja. I'll reason with him or my name isn't Arjun!" he says.

It is not quite daylight when Saroj Atya is awakened by a thundering on her door.

"Look what I've done! Look what I've done!" Gaja is screaming.

Muli slips under Bapusaheb's bed, out of sight.

Atya unbolts the door. Stale cigarette smoke invades the room when she opens it. She walks past Gaja into the sitting room. Linen, utensils, books, clothes, shoes are piled in crazy heaps on the floor.

"See! I've made it easier for you. Pack up now and leave!"

Gaja goes into the bedroom. "Where's Muli? Hiding is she? I'm going to fix your Laxmandriver, I am, once you're gone! That's right — I want you out too."

Atya runs to the Joshis' flat, rings the doorbell several times, hurries back leaving her front door wide open. She sits on the edge of Bapusaheb's bed, breathless. Muli remains out of sight.

"Start packing!" Gaja is impatient.

Atya points, "Look who's here!"

He quickly looks over his shoulder then stares at Atya. Standing behind him are Arjun, Arun, and Mr. Joshi.

Atya smothers a smile: the resolute look of the men — jaws dark green, bloodshot eyes bleary from interrupted sleep — is menacing. Just like the three hero-brothers in the film *Laal Aag*, Atya thinks, on their torrid mission to rescue the bosomy Sood sisters from the clutches of a multifarious gang of thieves, rapists, killers . . .

Gaja shakes off his momentary loss of composure and turns around. "You stay out of this, Arjun! This is a family matter!"

"Now it's Atya's turn is it?" Arjun asks.

"What!"

"You've swindled people for years, lived off them! What have you done this time Gaja, that you want Atya's flat? It must be a fat amount that you owe —"

"You keep out of this, Arjun. I've, I've never swindled —"

"Who do you think gave the Dancing Shiledar Family the two thousand rupees you owed them? Atya was out when they came collecting so Muli sent them to us. They said to tell you that unless you paid up within the week they'd set thugs on you. Do you know who got you out of that mess? Settled that debt? My father did but never told Atya about it. Spared her the humiliation —"

"What are you saying, Arjun?" Saroj Atya asks. But Arjun keeps looking at Gaja.

"You're talking nonsense!" Gaja says.

"Am I? But forget that: it's an old story. Atya tells me Vithoba came to you. In person. Well, He appeared to me, too, but being the simple fellow that I am, only in my dreams. Do you know what He told me Gaja? He said that you and I are to take part in a miracle! Yes! I'm to throw you off the verandah and He will catch you on your way down."

"Atya, tell them to leave the flat! He's, he's insulting me!"

Arjun motions for Atya not to move.

"So, are you ready, Gaja? I'll take Gaja's feet, Arun, you take his shoulders."

Arun and Arjun close in on Gaja. Mr. Joshi stands square in the doorway. He steps aside when Gaja staggers out the bedroom and out the front door.

"I don't think you're going to see him for a long time — What is it, Atya, why are you laughing?"

"Vithoba said a miracle would take place!" Atya is looking at Bapusaheb's face.

"But Atya!" says Arjun, thinking this Gaja business has finally unhinged her.

"Come and see! Look at Bapusaheb. He's doing it a second time!"

They quickly gather around the bed; Muli crawls out from under it.

Bapusaheb's twitching mouth stretches into a half-smile, stays like that for a couple of moments, relapses once again into comatose stillness.

After watching Muli adjust the oxygen tube that has slipped out of his nose, Atya walks slowly to her bed, removes a pair of diamond earrings from under her pillow. Slipping off her gold bangles, all six of them, she places her jewellery next to the marigold at Vithoba's feet.

I Am the Bougainvillaea

⁓

The first time Gopa sees Prem he's looking out the window, hands clasped behind his back, feet at ease. Military, she thinks, definitely. There must be at least fifty people here, all the occupants of her aunt and uncle's residential building. It is the wettest night of the monsoon season, and the rain is hurtling downwards in opaque blocks. Cars have been abandoned on the road, and it took Gopa a long time to get home this evening because she had to walk half a mile, shoes and sling bag held high above her head, the swirling, muddy eddies continuously thwarting her efforts to move forward.

There are many familiar faces but her gaze keeps returning to him. He is still turned away from her and she can see nothing now except the back of his head which is beginning to go bald at the top. He's not vain, she concludes, or wouldn't he have covered his thinning patch by combing some thick hair across it? She hears her name.

"There's someone I want you to meet," her aunt, Latamavshi, says. Gopa knows right away it's going to be the military man.

"Prem, I want you to meet my niece, Gopa."

"Namaskar!" he says. Large, flat palms and slim, long fingers make a graceful cone as they join together in greeting.

"Namaskar!" A surgeon, she changes her mind, definitely.

"Prem is an old classmate of your uncle. His car got stalled at the traffic lights so he came in to make a phone call. I insisted he stay for dinner. Oh! Hello Hemi . . ." Her aunt turns to another guest.

Gopa joins Prem at the window. Its wooden frame is leaking and already there are puddles the length of it. Peering through the glass at distant smudged lights, a thought begins to take shape: It's just him and me and the blunt sound of the rain as it cleanses the city, the people behind us insubstantial as their melting reflections in the windowpane.

Prem is watching her closely. "What?" she blurts out.

Prem laughs. "How much longer are you going to be in Bombay?" he asks.

He knows more about her than she does about him.

"Another week," she says.

"You will meet my son then. He's arriving tomorrow." Gopa detects a triumphant tone that indicates there's been a battle somewhere along the line. And then it dawns on her that Latamavshi is trying to matchmake again.

"From where?"

"The States. Ram has lived abroad for a number of years but this time he's coming home for good."

Gopa's heard similar optimism before. Parents hoping their sons will return home and provide them with grandchildren so there may be some brightness in their fading years.

"Are you sure he's coming to stay?" It's none of her business but tonight she doesn't hesitate to say what comes to mind.

"Well then, we must make sure, mustn't we?"

She nods without thinking.

Many months later, watching a small sheaf of wheat rise and fall to a rhythm that matches her own, a brief thought will dart in and out of her head: I met the father and said "yes" to the son.

Now, looking at Prem's smooth, flat palms, she decides: if ever I fall sick and need a knife, I'll go to him, definitely.

Gopa meets Ram the following day. She expects a short, stout, dark-skinned individual because Latamavshi has told her that Ram is very different from his father, but she is pleasantly surprised. Ram is thin, tall, with a not quite fair but then again not so dark complexion.

He says little when they are introduced, but Gopa barely registers his reserved manner because Prem makes sure there are no awkward silences. His work as interior decorator — not a surgeon, after all — brings him into contact with the privileged janata and he regales Gopa and Ram with detailed stories about his clients. Ram is not even remotely acquainted with the Bollywood scene, yet even he enjoys listening to his father describe "star" homes that imitate lavish film sets; homes with acres and acres of plush red carpeting, winding staircases that twist and turn, mammoth chandeliers the kind under which the besotted hero seduces his heroine by singing maudlin love songs. Gopa, an avid filmgoer, is enthralled. By the time she is ready to leave, she concludes the last six days of her holidays have been the best, definitely.

Within weeks of returning home to Satara, Gopa's parents receive a proposal for her hand in marriage. The letter is written by Prem. Even though her parents have not met any of the Gupte family, they have made detailed enquiries into their credentials ever since Gopa and Latamavshi told them about Prem's hospitality and his reasons for it. They have heard nothing objectionable; they tell Gopa she is free to make up her mind.

She considers the proposal with the same seriousness with which she considered other proposals in the past. She turned those eligibles down because she couldn't bring herself to say yes to any of them. Gopa accepts Ram now simply because she cannot say no.

They are married shortly afterwards. Gopa's parents wish to have the wedding in Satara but Ram wants it held in Bombay. He insists that there be no honeymoon as he doesn't want to take time off work. Friends and family laughingly urge him to make the time; later on there will be none, they argue. But Ram's mind is made up. His face closes in when the topic is mentioned and he makes himself so remote that Gopa hasn't the nerve to bring it up herself.

"I don't know whether Ram has told you," Prem says to Gopa one evening when they are standing on the balcony, waiting for Ram to come home. "This Maya Building flat is my wedding gift to you both."

Gopa shakes her head. "Ram didn't say anything," she says and smiles her thanks. She points to a potted bougainvillaea that fans one end of the wall. She is struck by its vibrant magenta so unusual in a polluted city where flowers bloom in washed-out hues. "What's the secret?" she asks Prem. "What special ingredient do you add to the soil that makes the leaves so bright?"

"No secret. It's always looked like that," he says, glancing at his watch. "What's keeping Ram? I was hoping to eat early tonight." Prem leaves for his farm at five o'clock the next morning. Raising chickens in Khopoli has always been his retirement dream.

"I can serve dinner right away."

"No, no. We'll wait," Prem says. "And, before I forget, there is no need for you to see me off tomorrow."

Gopa nods, watching the sun settle itself into the curving horizon.

The next morning she wakes to find Ram bathed and dressed and eating breakfast.

"I'm sorry," Gopa says. "You should have woken me up."

"What for?"

"Well, I could have made you something to eat —"

"There's no need, Gopa. You don't have to wait on me, you know. I'm not used to that!"

Gopa hurries to the kitchen, puts some water on to boil. She reaches for the tea leaves but try as she might she cannot get Ram's expression out of her mind: *You don't have to wait on me.* The thought of tea is suddenly unpalatable and she turns off the stove. Ram enters the kitchen and rinses his breakfast things in the basin. "I'm off," he says. "See you this evening."

"Do you know what time you'll be back?" she asks. He shakes his head.

Gopa bolts the front door and goes in for her bath. Afterwards, she circles tall house plants standing upright in polished brass urns, caresses shining leaves that give the rooms their garden-like verdancy.

Ram has told her that she can decorate the flat to her taste, rearrange the furniture if she wants. The only thing he doesn't want is for her to engage servants. "If I can take care of myself, my things, so can you, Gopa." It's not the housework that bothers her; what hurts is Ram's authoritarian manner, his complete disregard for what *she* wants. And, having no servants means she has the flat to herself. Her parents' house pulses with life and silent rooms make her feel hollow. She spends a large part of her day standing on the balcony, envying the people who are going somewhere, who have some place to go to.

A voice that says, "Surely this isn't the way it's supposed to be," is as yet too faint to be heard.

One afternoon, she gets lost while trying to post a letter and finds the Gangadhar School for the Blind. She enters to get directions and on an impulse applies to be a voluntary reader. She is surprised and delighted by the enthusiasm with which she is greeted.

Starting that day, she goes to the Gangadhar School three times a week and can barely hold back her tears afterwards as she makes her way home. Overwhelmed by the children's ability to face perpetual darkness, her heart twists every time she visualizes the bird-like movement of their heads, necks craning forward as they listen to her read. After the first week she gently removes the dark glasses that some of them wear and is relieved when the children seem not to miss them. The shades have no function except to protect us from their vacant, opaque eyes, Gopa thinks, and we don't need protection.

Ram is very pleased that she is doing something useful.

Some days Gopa visits her aunt and uncle. Gopa and Ram are often invited there to dinner but rarely go because Ram is never too keen. "But that doesn't mean you can't go," he says to her. "Keep the driver for the evening."

A few times Ram doesn't return home from work until the early hours of the morning. The first time Gopa phones him, she speaks only after making sure her tone is clear of accusation, her voice clean of tears. She apologizes for calling and explains that she was worried. "That's all right," he says, "I'll be home soon, go to sleep." But it's a long time before she hears his key in the front door.

Ram keeps in close touch with his school friends, some of whom are unmarried. Sometimes they get invited to his married friends' homes. One evening they meet a new couple.

Aru Kopkar has dark, arched eyebrows and long, black hair that hangs down one side of her face like a velvet screen. Ram replenishes her gin and tonic, offers to fill her dinner plate, laughs loudly at all her jokes. She has a considerable collection and a certain knack for telling them, Gopa has to admit. But she fervently wishes Ram would be more circumspect as she tries not to watch them from across the room — Aru running tapering fingers over shining hair as though plucking the strings of a silk-spun harp, Ram wearing an expression Gopa has never had the privilege of evoking.

The evening finally comes to an end and Gopa, realizing that Ram has left ahead of her, hurries outside. She finds him in conversation with Aru, hears him ask for her phone number. Aru's husband is standing nearby looking very bored and equally smug. He's used to others fawning over his wife, Gopa thinks, and the thought is suddenly comforting. But everything within her cringes as she slips into their car. She starts it and Ram gets in.

Gopa doesn't know what becomes of Ram asking Aru for her phone number, and when they all meet at subsequent dinners he is still attentive to her, but not as besotted as that first time. Gopa keeps an eye on Aru's husband, waits for any sign that will give her a clue that something is amiss, and having observed him carefully decides that nothing is. Gopa says nothing to Ram about Aru. What's to say? And perhaps because all the women Gopa has ever known have stood up and faced life without turning their backs, she now does the same: she refuses to buckle under the weight of her own reality, to run away, to leave.

"What do you think of the way I look?" she asks Ram after dinner one evening, when the Aru incident has temporarily receded to the back of her mind.

"Your hair needs combing in the front." Ram doesn't look up from his book.

"I didn't mean that," Gopa says, pulling back and tucking the loose strands into her bun.

"Sorry . . . what?"

"Do you find me attractive?"

He says yes, but she doubts his sincerity.

"On a scale of one to ten what am I?"

"Five."

She knows she shouldn't have asked. It matters not a bit that she is complimented on her looks by almost everyone she meets. What matters is that he has confirmed what she has suspected all along: he thinks I'm average and who in their right mind would want to touch an average person?

Her nights are long and restless. The only time she sleeps well is when Ram is out of town and she doesn't have to figure out his mood at bedtime: will he, won't he? And when he gets into bed beside her, switches off the light, and quickly falls asleep, she curls away from him, clings to the edge of the mattress and repeats: I am like the bougainvillaea on the balcony. Wind, rain, or smog, I survive. It becomes a mantra. I am like the bougainvillaea.

One Monday morning while he is getting dressed, Ram tells her, "I'm going away on Thursday."

"That's short notice," Gopa says. "Where are you going?"

"To my ten-year class reunion." He pats aftershave on his cheeks.

"Oh! Not a business trip, then. How long will you be gone?" Gopa asks, straightening the razai.

"Don't know yet — I'll be late coming home tonight. I have to go to a client's house to see the layout."

That night, when they're in bed, she puts her arm around him and asks rather tentatively, "Can I come with you to your class reunion?"

"Of course not."

"Why not?"

"It's not possible."

"Why not? Other wives will be there, won't they?"

"I suppose so, but what's that got to do with anything?"

"So why can't I come? I'd like to see your old school . . ."

"I told you: it's not possible!"

"Oh please!"

She hugs him tighter. He turns on his side, opens a book.

"No. I'm staying with RK and his flat is very small."

"Maybe we can stay with the Raos," she says to his back.

"No!"

"Why not?"

"I've already written to RK. He called this morning — everything is arranged."

"You've known about the reunion for a while. Why didn't you tell me before?" Gopa turns away from his back.

"Oh, don't go on and on. I didn't think it was important. Now go to sleep!"

She doesn't bring up the topic again.

Ram travels frequently and she always packs his suitcase. Not this time. He doesn't ask her to and the next evening he packs it himself. He leaves for the reunion and is back Sunday night. The following morning he is in a hurry to get to work.

After having spent the entire weekend debating whether she will do anything for Ram any more, Gopa decides that this one time she will make an exception. She will unpack his suitcase. She lays it flat on the floor, carries the used clothing to the bathroom.

When she is removing the rest of his clothes she finds it, right at the bottom of the suitcase, carefully wedged between two clean shirts: a letter, severely but neatly creased as though it had been folded into the smallest package possible. One that would fit into a wallet compartment, Gopa thinks. It is addressed to Ram. The writer, Meera, is an old, intimate friend of Ram's who was with him at university in the States. Gopa reads the paragraph at the end over and over again: *"I know life has changed for you dramatically since we last met. Rekha wrote me in New York. I thought about calling you a million times but — it's no use thinking about that. I really want to see you. And now that Rekha tells me you are coming, I just can't wait."*

Gopa wonders whether this is the woman he was in love with abroad, before things went wrong between them and caused him to return to India, where he married the first girl he was introduced to. This would explain his indifference, his remoteness, his lack of feeling, she thinks. She empties the suitcase on the bed, throws his clothes into various drawers and barely stops herself from shredding the loosely written piece of paper along its myriad creases.

That evening Gopa opens the door to Ram as soon as she hears his footsteps on the landing. "Where did this come from?" she demands, brandishing the letter.

He stops in the doorway, takes his time replying. "It's from before I married you. I found it when I opened the case." He walks past her and sits on the sofa in the living room.

"You didn't. You've used this suitcase before," Gopa says, slumping into the armchair across from him.

"So?"

"It wasn't there before. I always pack."

"It's from before. Besides, she's married now."

"That's why you didn't want me to come with you — and

94

what's that supposed to mean: she's married now?" Gopa says, untwisting her hair from its bun, re-twisting it into a tighter roll.

He doesn't answer her. She has no choice but to let the matter drop. There is no year in the upper right-hand corner, only the day and the month. She goes to the kitchen, lights the stove, and watches the letter burn to ashes.

Afterwards, when dinner is ready, she calls out to Ram. He doesn't answer so she goes and stands in the doorway of their bedroom.

"I'm not hungry," he says, without looking up from his book.

She has never seen him so tense. She clears the table and eats some rice and curds on the balcony. Later, when she gets into bed, he says nothing. In the morning he is silent. He's acting as if he's the injured party, she thinks bitterly. I should be the one to stop talking to him. So she does.

Three nights later Gopa breaks the silence. She's been getting headaches for a while now but the tension between them is giving her migraines.

"Are you awake?" she asks.

"I was just falling asleep. What is it?" He is turned away from her.

"It's been three weeks," she mutters.

"What's been three — tomorrow. I'm too tired. Go to sleep now."

"Just a cuddle then."

"Uh-uh!"

"Come on . . ."

"All right, just for two minutes. I have an important meeting in the morning."

She snuggles against his back. Wants to make the two minutes last forever, to stretch them into something more.

"Please . . ."

"Don't push me!"

"I'm not staying on that stupid old pill any more. Why bother anyway —"

"Don't —"

"— makes me nauseous, bloats me up —"

"It's two minutes now. Go to sleep."

It's no use. Ram continues to shut her out and her headaches persist. When she sees a doctor she is surprised to learn that she has high blood pressure. No one in her family has this tendency. Dr. Natu instructs her to stop taking the pill.

That night, when Gopa tells Ram about her visit to Dr. Natu, he asks, "Why didn't you tell me you were getting headaches?"

"I did."

"What did the doctor say?"

"He says that I have high blood pressure."

"Oh?"

"He thinks it's the pill. Doesn't want me to take it any more."

There's no reaction from Ram and Gopa thinks: he doesn't care, it won't bother him if he never touches me again.

"Why are you so upset?" he asks. "It only means we'll have children earlier than planned."

Earlier? Planned? The only time the subject has been mentioned was before the wedding, when he told her quietly, in a room full of people, "Make sure you go on the pill before we're married." She looked at him, unsure of what she'd heard.

"You understand? Yes?" His voice had been gentle. She nodded agreement.

Ram says no more. Gopa knows he is not teasing or deliberately misleading her by mentioning children now; that is not in his nature. She wants to ask him to elaborate, wants to discuss the possibilities of starting a family. But the letter incident is still so fresh in her mind that she is determined not to respond to the slight thaw she detects in his manner. And now that she's off the pill she's determined not to be too optimistic about having children, which is just as well because nothing in that direction happens.

Late one afternoon when Ram is away on business, Gopa comes home from the Institute to find Prem waiting outside her front door. She guesses the purpose of his visit the minute she sees him: he is here for Ram's birthday.

"You should have phoned and let me know what time you were arriving so I could have stayed home!" she says, unlocking the door. "I've planned a surprise party for Ram tomorrow night."

"I thought you would have. That's why I'm here!" he smiles, following her into the living room. "Also, life is about to get very hectic at the farm so I thought I'd come to Bombay before the busy season begins. As it is, I can only stay a couple of nights."

"Would you like a cup of tea?"

"Yes," he nods, "I'll just put my bag in the spare room."

Gopa hasn't seen Prem in a long while; he rarely comes to the city and every time Gopa suggests they go to the farm, Ram is never very keen. He says he dislikes the badly maintained state highways, the single lanes, the crater-like potholes.

Gopa is genuinely pleased to see Prem today. He's never felt like a father-in-law; more like a family friend. He takes her to Bertorelli's for an early dinner. Afterwards, they go to the airport to fetch Ram. He is not on the incoming flight. Gopa is quiet on the drive home.

The phone rings just as she is turning off her bedside lamp. She fumbles for the receiver. It's Ram, calling to say he won't be coming tonight, that the meeting ran on longer than expected.

"I'll be home Sunday," he says. "I tried getting a seat on tomorrow's flight but everything is booked."

"It's your birthday tomorrow," she whispers.

"My birthday, not yours," he laughs. "I tried to call you earlier."

"We were out —"

"I'll see you day after."

"Yes." Things are never going to change, she tells herself, no matter what. Why do I even bother trying?

There's a knock on her door. Prem is silhouetted against the light in the hallway. He comes and sits in the armchair next to her bed, reaches for the lamp.

"Don't turn it on!" Gopa sits up and rubs her face with her hands.

"I thought you were asleep so I picked up the phone when it rang! What is the matter with the boy? He was always quiet but never this aloof, this distant. I shouldn't have let him go to the States. I know that now. His mother's death was a great shock to all of us. Here one day, gone the next. So close they were. After her death I told Ram to postpone his leaving home but he kept saying sticking to his university plans is what his mother would have wanted. She had an instinct about him, you know. Knew how to handle —"

"His mother was probably the only person who did. You don't and I — I never will," Gopa's voice is resigned. From now on Ram will be just someone I happen to share the house with, she decides. He can do what he wants and nothing he does will ever affect me.

"No, don't say that. Patience is what you need to deal with my son, Gopa, infinite patience," Prem says. "You'll see, one day he will realize that you are good for him. It takes time for him to get used to things, to adjust. He's always been like that."

Gopa is pushing back the cuticles on her fingernails, intent on uncovering the sunken moons. Why did he marry me? Why? The question is an acrid refrain.

"At first, when I suggested he return and take over my business he said, 'Forget it.' Then one day, he called me from New York and said he was ready to return. Just like that! And you know how hard he works. Once he's committed to something, he'll give it his best. You just need patience, Gopa, that's all.

"I was optimistic, you know, when I first saw you. You looked beautiful with your damp hair and quick smile. I liked your confidence too. He'll fall in love with her, I thought. What's not to love? And come to think of it, Ram must have thought so too, otherwise why would he have agreed to marry you? But there is no harm in asserting yourself, Gopa. Why did you not tell him about tomorrow night, about all the trouble you have taken to arrange the party? Why don't you stand up for yourself? Where is the girl who used to say 'definitely' with such conviction?"

Her eyes are dark, swollen, streaming. He moves forward in his chair. "I'm sorry," he says over and over again. "I shouldn't have said that. Of course it's not your fault. It's his."

Anything he says, any kind words, only make her cry more. He urges her to lie down, to rest. Taking her hands in his, he tells her that things will seem better in the morning.

She does not listen to him, will not let go of his hands. She notices a small birthmark, a rounded sheaf of wheat that lies in the hollow pool of his throat. She reaches up and rests a finger in that hollow. His eyes are wide-spaced and liquid and his hands are warm when he touches her neck.

In the middle of the night when she reaches across he is still there beside her. She moves nearer and places her face against his back; he turns and takes her in his arms.

When she next awakens, glaring sunshine covers her bed. She recoils, shuts her eyes. What have I done? How could I? What now? There's a knock on the door. She panics, pulls the counterpane up to her chin. The door opens slightly and Prem says, "I heard you stir. There's tea on the table. I'm just making toast."

His tone is normal, unchanged. She jumps out of bed. I imagined everything, she thinks. But by the time she joins Prem at the table she knows what happened last night happened.

"Help yourself." He barely looks up from the newspaper. That's normal as well. When it comes to reading, father and son are identical in their ability to be totally absorbed.

Having decided to go ahead with the party, Gopa is in a hurry to get started for the day. When she comes back from the kitchen, Prem is folding the newspaper. He puts it down and looks up at her. His gaze is as firm as always.

"I hope you're not thinking of cancelling tonight?"

Gopa shakes her head.

"Good! I could drive you to the vegetable market."

"That's okay," Gopa says, "I have the driver today."

He unfolds the paper, goes back to where he left it.

Gopa smiles. She does not think of Prem or Ram or about what happened last night. Instead she remembers visits to her parents' home in Satara. She goes there mostly when Ram is out of town on business trips. As she approaches Satara it is as though her marriage never happened and when she returns to Ram she feels whole again, rejuvenated. This morning it's a similar feeling.

Ram arrives in Bombay on the afternoon flight. He doesn't call beforehand and Gopa doesn't know whether to laugh or cry when he walks through the front door and thrusts a brown-paper package into her hands. His very first present to her. That night she wears her new magenta silk with emerald-green border.

Bright sunshine is crawling up the foot of her bed. Gopa sits up and looks into the mirror on the opposite wall. She rolls her hands over her stomach to gauge its size, then turns sideways. Everything looks the same except my face, she notes, my skin is glowing, my mouth is more defined, the puffiness around my eyes is gone.

It is not until after she's eaten breakfast that she remembers she is alone. Normally this thought would have kept her company day and night. Lately she feels detached, unconnected, her immediate life as remote as the movement of distant planets around another sun.

Tonight, she tells herself, when I fetch Ram at the airport I will have something to tell him.

He is waiting for her outside the terminal building. He looks tired, his face is tanned and drawn. "Short business trips, yes. But from now on I get someone else . . . ," he says, getting into the car.

When they reach home he asks, "What is it?"

"What?" she says, turning to face him, tucking a loose strand of hair behind her ear.

"Is there something you want to tell me?"

"You noticed!"

"Well? Are you going to tell me or not?"

He's different, she thinks. Ever since he gave me that present, something's changed. Or maybe it's just me. Yes, it's me. And suddenly, she has to tell him right away. He puts down his suitcase. He has heard all right. She can tell by the look in his eyes, now so alert, so renewed.

She turns away, walks out on the balcony. He comes and leans against the railing next to her. "See those kerosene lanterns on the fishing boats?" he says. "My mother used to say they reminded her of the jewels the sea must have tossed up when the world was created." She looks to where he is pointing but all she can see is a tiny being with flat, smooth palms and long, slim fingers joined together in exquisite greeting.

End the Journey

I narrowed my eyes, focused my gaze on the object floating towards me. It looked like a tightly constructed boat made of dried leaves, similar to the woven baskets used by worshippers to carry votive offerings to Lakshmi-Narayan: aromatic garlands for prayers answered, scarlet hibiscus for sufferings relieved, marigold strings for problems solved. I tucked the front of my sari between my legs and crouched at the edge of the sea. The greenish-brown boat sailed right into my hands. I held it to my face; clean, clear water was caught inside.

"Throw it back, Tara!" Kunda was staring down at me, the rims of her nostrils flushed pink, sunlight shining through the tops of her ears. "Throw it back!" Her voice was on the ascendant, shrill, helpless, a slight-boned bird in a cross-current of warring winds. "Don't you know that . . . that thing must have floated down from the cremation ghats?" People paused in their morning walk and looked at us with curiosity. But when they realized that no madman had grabbed a beckoning breast, no thief had snatched a glinting chain, they slowly moved away.

Kunda shuddered and turned on her heels when I emptied the boat on the sand. She was probably admonishing herself not to think about the flowers it might have carried, the ones meant for a dead body. I stood up quickly, tucked the boat into the waist of my sari where its keel dug into my skin. The queasy feeling I had woken to that morning returned.

Crossing our main road we saw Kamat Kaki swaying towards us, spindly bow legs perfectly curved brackets, nine-yard sari worn higher than usual so as not to soil it on the seashore.

We met at the traffic light. "Kasa kay. Theek?" She beamed at me, then looked sideways at Kunda, no doubt to assess what was written in that porcelain skin this morning. A red flush was sweeping down Kunda's nose.

"Shouldn't be out in this cool, fresh air, Kunda," Kamat Kaki said. "Want to catch pneumonia or what? Ask your cook to make gauti kadha. Before you know it all knotted phlegm will be loose." Kaki winked at me as Kunda hurried past, face averted.

"Too thin, Tara!" Her eyes swept my body. "Married one year but . . . Arvind is doing his duty or what? I bought some fresh surmai from the fish-boy this morning. Come later on, at ten o' clock and I'll show you what masala to apply. You want to learn how to prepare fish, yes or no?"

The walk sign turned green. I nodded, smiled at Kamat Kaki, followed my sister-in-law, Kunda, home.

Arvind was buttoning his shirt in front of the mirror when I entered our room, tray in hand, Moti following close behind me. I set it down on the bed, handed Arvind his bowl of pohay.

"Sit, Moti," I ordered. "Don't move!" But he ignored me and wagging his tail coiled himself on the balcony in the sun.

"What is that?" Arvind asked when he saw me remove the boat from my waist. I held it up. It was bent and cracked. He took it from me, straightened its keel and sides and placed it on his night table.

"It sailed right to me," I said. "I had to bring it home."

Arvind pointed to a cardboard shoebox on the dressing

table. "Isn't it time you returned some of those seashells to the sea?" he smiled, picking up his bowl of pohay.

I rubbed my palms against my crumpled sari, dropped my eyes. Who could have predicted that one day I would be here in his house, amongst his people: his parents, child-like twin sister Manda, younger sister Kunda, still the baby of the family in spite of her twenty-five years? That one day I would share this unmade bed I was sitting on, the imprints of our heads etched into flattened pillows, the contours of our bodies under the ridges of the unstraightened razai? An incongruent pair we must have made on our wedding day: he, milk fair, grey eyed, tall and broad, whereas I, dark skinned, nose without a bridge, hair so thick and unmanageable that it required fifty pins to hold it down. What does he see in me, what did he see in me, that first time at my uncle's house in Calcutta? Me, who was so certain I would marry a widower or at the very least a middle-aged man because I was twenty-eight and already four boys had rejected my large hands, sun-charred skin, shaky voice.

And then, after that first meeting, before I could register the sweep of Arvind's wide forehead, the golden-yellow point in the centre of his sapphire ring, the widening of his nostrils when he smiled, I was rescued from my own predictions. But pessimism being tightly embroidered into the spine of my consciousness, I couldn't keep myself from mumbling to him on the night of our wedding, a sudden urge pushing me to get rid of that constant companion of a thought that rattled inside my head: "You shouldn't have married me. I won't be able to make you happy."

He'd taken my hand. "And why not? What is it that you think you cannot give me that will make me happy?"

I hadn't expected this calm question. My version of this scene had him answering ponderously, relief weighing down

105

his voice and tone: All right, if that's the way you feel, we'll live like brother and sister. So I said the first thing that came into my mind, the one thing I wanted more than anything in the world and therefore assumed I could not have. "Children," I whispered, hoping he wouldn't notice the dampness of my palms.

"Why ever not? Do you not have a regular cycle?"

My eyes were fixed on the Cinthol calendar, on the blissful mother hugging two laughing children to her breast, cresting waves of fine hair rising up on their small, delicate heads. So I caught his teasing tone but missed the twinkle in his eye.

A month later, long after we'd returned from our honeymoon in Mahableshwar where the weather had turned from damp to cool to sunny, I asked Kunda why she thought her brother had married me. She shrugged, muttering that she didn't have a clue considering he'd rejected so many eligible girls in the past.

I mulled over this information for a few days and like a brown-winged moth who leaves the warm, embracing shadows of the night to go in search of a burning bulb, I approached Kunda one afternoon, asked her to tell me about those girls in his past.

She didn't ask why I wanted to know, what good my knowing would do. I suppose she thought it natural that I would be puzzled by Arvind's choice. After all, there was no denying the improbable had happened. A highly qualified boy coming from a well-known family had said yes to a girl who was not only an orphan, but the progeny of a plain-looking stock. Perhaps the very same question had crossed Kunda's mind: Why *did* Arvind say yes to Tara?

"Their names," I demanded, "the expressions on their faces, the colour of their skins, the shapes of their noses." My desire to get to the bottom fuelling Kunda's willingness to tell me all. So I couldn't blame her, not afterwards, when their fair, graceful forms ravaged my head.

Rekha, the dimpled, round-faced daughter of a retired I.A.S. officer who wore hipster saris, who would have planned fashionable dinner parties for Arvind and their friends, buffet table laden with fresh-fried pompret, prawn curry, kokum saar, cashew nut burfi, sweet wheat kheer, creamy mango ice cream. Who would have invited her parents and their influential friends home so that Arvind would have been persuaded to leave the small cardboard factory that employed him to work for an international shipping company, some prestigious import-export firm, a big chain of five-star hotels.

Or he would now be knotting his tie in front of Kunda's best friend, Sheela, who plucked her eyebrows so fine that she had to colour them back in with an eyebrow pencil. Sheels, as Kunda called her, whom I had met because she visited every now and then, doctor husband in tow, slightly protruding teeth lending an endearing, child-like quality to her smile. Sheela would have gone up to Arvind — not sat on the bed tongue-tied, wiping damp palms against crumpled sheets — laughingly removed his tie, chosen another one in a deeper blue to heighten the greyness in his eyes.

Or it could have been Mona, Arvind's second cousin. Yes, Kunda hadn't spared me the cousin who had rejected *him*, Arvind. The cousin whom he had loved from the moment he'd first set eyes on her in the cradle (if I could get carried away with my questions then I couldn't deny Kunda her tendency for dramatic mirchi-masala), and who had promised herself to Arvind until she met a certain boy on a holiday in Darjeeling. I didn't dare ask for Mona's description, but I imagined her snub-nosed, haughty-chinned, smug-faced . . . beautiful. With long, flowing limbs and even longer nails. I could see her now, running them over Arvind's suit jacket, an easy familiarity in her manner because she had known him from childhood. She wouldn't have brought a cracked boat home. No, she and Kunda would have scoured the shore for the perfect seashell and, finding it, would have carried it carefully, heedless of Kamat Kaki's greeting at the traffic light. Once home, she would have asked Kunda to bathe it in the basin, and stood over her all the time urging, "harder, harder, rub it harder!" until she was satisfied that its pink inside gleamed like mother-of-pearl. Then, late at night, when the only other presence in the room was the perfect crescent of a waxing moon, Mona would have laid it on her pillow and she and Arvind would have put their heads together, listened to the gentle lapping of the waves —

"Hold Moti back, will you, Tara? Or he'll chew my tie. Where are you this morning? I asked how the walk with Kunda went at least three times."

"All right, until I picked up that boat." I restrained Moti by his collar. He sat back easily on my feet.

"As long as you learn to ignore her nervousness . . . I spoke to the professor last night. He finally agrees that it's high time he and Ma stop rejecting every boy that is proposed for her. Kunda may be fragile but nothing is wrong with her health, nothing that a normal married life won't cure — You better take Moti away, Tara, or he'll jump on me the minute you release him."

I shut Moti in Manda's room and went to the kitchen to place Arvind's lunch box in his briefcase.

After he left for the office, I ran to the balcony, watched him get into his white Fiat. When his car passed through the traffic light, I turned to the mogra creeper. Its thick buds were lit by the morning sun. I plucked several and dropped them into the palms of my hands. When I could hold no more, I stepped back into the room, placed them carefully on my dressing table.

I went to the kitchen, ate a banana. I hoped it would relieve the slightly queasy feeling that still lined my stomach, the residue, no doubt, of the coconut oil the cook had used in the Goan kadhi last night.

I turned on the geyser in the bathroom and while the buckets were being filled, I made our bed, and then uncoiled my hair from its loosened bun.

Afterwards, when I was draping my sari, I put my hands to my nose. The sweet smell of mogra hadn't washed away.

As I stood on the balcony, combing out my wet hair, I could hear Kunda practising her singing in the sitting room. I called out to the cook and asked him to make me a cup of tea when he made one for Kunda. When I finished dotting my forehead, I went and sat on the sofa opposite her. She placed her hand on the strings of the tambora, laid it sideways across her lap. Giving me a half-smile, she dabbed her brow with a handker-chief. The bones in her throat moved delicately as she sipped hot tea.

"Don't exert yourself too much, Kundababy!" the professor called from the dining room. His voice was thick, throaty.

"I'm not, Baba. Tara and I are drinking tea."

"It's just that I don't want you exhausted at the beginning of the day. Continue now, let me hear your sweet voice."

Kunda opened her song book. I went to see Arvind's mother in her bedroom.

"Kundababy is making real progress!" she exclaimed, as soon as she saw me standing in the doorway, "the professor is so pleased." She was lying down.

I sat at the foot of her bed. "How are you this morning?" I asked, massaging her feet.

"You know how it is, Tara," she sighed, rubbing her right shoulder. "Every time I sleep on my right side I face this problem. Last night — even though he's told me a hundred times not to — I was on my right side, watching the door, waiting for the professor to come home. I must have fallen asleep while I was waiting and now it's so sore —"

"Let me massage your arm," I said.

She patted my hand, closed her eyes, hummed along with Kunda who was now singing a prayer. She was a handsome woman, her beauty more sturdy, less fragile than her daughter's, the nights the professor had not returned home etched into the dark crescents under her eyes, the grey mornings when she'd woken to an odour of stale whisky, dyed into her hair.

"That feels better," she said, after two minutes. "Now see if Kundababy needs fresh water, and give her this clean hand-kerchief."

Kunda was singing a thumri, her fingers moving over the upright tambora. She didn't look at me. I went to Manda's room. It was empty. I leaned over the railing of her balcony. Manda was walking inside the compound; Moti was running circles around her, bounding along the compound wall when he sensed the presence of another dog on the other side. Sakubai, the woman who had been specially hired to take care of Manda, looked up and saw me. She said something to Manda, pointing upwards. Manda tipped back her head and waved, a female version of Arvind with his heavy-lidded eyes, rounded jaw, wide mouth. I waved back. After a minute I went to my room for I knew that as long as I stood on the balcony, Manda would continue to look up at me.

I gathered the mogra buds and sewing box from my dressing table, sat on the bed. I threaded the thinnest needle. After spreading the buds out on the razai, I pushed the stem of the smallest into the needle's sharp tip, envisioning the garland which I knew would blossom by evening. I could hear Moti's barking, Manda's delighted giggles, her universe reduced to the here and now, present obliterating the past, completely oblivious of the future. That's the way it was with Manda.

My mind started ticking: if only my todays weren't tainted by my yesterdays, if only my todays weren't . . .

I'd have no memory of my Calcutta aunt.

"You should have stuck to the pattern, Taru," she would say. "See how those puffed sleeves stand up. The original pattern had regular sleeves, didn't it?" And I would turn red, the diminutive of my name not deceiving me the least into believing that she cared for me.

"It's too soft. You should have added more sugar," she'd lick her fingers lustily, addressing the cook who was standing behind her, rolling his eyes at the servant who held the silver platter containing a fresh batch of sweetmeats.

My Calcutta uncle wasn't spared either. "I kept trying to get your attention but you never once looked my way. We should have left the wedding half an hour earlier. Then we would have missed the Durga procession. Everyone yelling out those bhajans, those dancing bodies — they make my head ache."

It was the same with her friends. "I think, Banoo, this chicken would have been perfect if you'd asked my driver to fetch it from the market. He's good you know — those people eat everything: mutton, chicken, fish, even beef — has this ekdum uncanny knack for knowing what will turn out tender."

And I wouldn't remember the desolation I felt when Vinayak Kaka had his final heart attack, here, in Bombay. Nor hear his laboured wheezing, each breath clawing its way down collapsing lungs; nor see the street lamps like some ghostly watering cans pelting giant drops of rain, drowning us all in helplessness.

Meera Kaku crouching in the corner of Vinayak Kaka's room, her eyes streaming, the end of her sari held tightly against her mouth; Shaila, her small head heavy on my lap as we waited on the divan, our eyes glued on the ticking clock; Shaila's mother, soaking, running in and out of the rain, searching the house for the right medication, while outside the roads resembled a rising sea through which no ambulance could navigate. And I wouldn't remember Shaila's father say to her mother that Vinayak Kaka's cremation was the longest he ever attended because there was not a single piece of dry wood to be found in the city. Wouldn't remember the grey dreams that haunted me afterwards, dreams of a damp, sluggish funeral pyre.

And if indeed, like Manda's, my present were to neatly overlap with my past, I wouldn't remember the worst time of all: the final days of my beloved grandmother, bed sores pouring foully onto her already stained sheets, the twisting pain in her groin. "Your Calcutta uncle must take care of you, your Calcutta uncle must take care of you, but so many years have passed since I met him, no, no, let Vinayak Kaka know, promise me you will write to him the minute I die, he will do the necessary, he is to be trusted." All the time stroking my face, my hair, my hands, the only caresses I remembered and knew.

Kunda was standing in the doorway. "That was Kamat Kaki on the phone. She said she's waiting for you."

I looked down, willing myself to swallow the wetness in my eyes. I ran my hand over the razai; there were no buds left. I bit off the thread, returned the needle to its place then coiled the garland on my palm. "What time is it, Kunda?" My voice was steady.

"You don't have to go to Kamat Kaki's if you don't want, you know. She's just taking advantage of your good nature, Tara. Just because she doesn't have anyone to talk to since her daughter got married . . ." Kunda shook her head. "It's five past ten."

"Already? I'll be back soon, Kunda, but in case I'm not, make sure Sakubai gives Manda her lunch at eleven-thirty. If we're not strict with Bai, Manda will go hungry —"

"She'll do nothing of the kind. What do you think? That she was starving before you married my brother?"

I finished running a comb over my head and looked at Kunda. The rims of her nostrils, the tops of her ears were smooth alabaster. I smiled as I handed her the garland. She sniffed it then tucked it into the top of her plait. "Go then, if you must, Tara, but come back in time for Manda's lunch. If you think I'm going to tell Bai what to do! Manda and I are the only two people she smiles at in this house and that's because we stay out of her way!" Grinning, Kunda walked me to the front door.

I had to cross the road to get to Kamat Kaki's house. The intersection was choked with traffic. I manoeuvred my way between hooting cars.

By the time I reached her landing, my legs felt weighted down with lead. I was shaking them vigorously when Kaki opened the front door.

She scrutinized me from under her eyebrows, eyes moving up and down my body.

"Legs feel heavy?" she asked.

"How did you guess, Kaki!"

"Never mind. Was the steep flight of stairs too tiring for you? You can lie down on the sofa if you want."

"At ten in the morning?" I laughed.

"Yet my stairs have never given you a problem before." She obviously expected some kind of explanation but I didn't have any. Besides, whatever was weighing them down before had now disappeared.

I followed her into the kitchen.

113

On the table, neatly laid out on a shining pink formica top was a large knot of ginger, a slightly less than equal quantity of peeled garlic, fresh coriander and chopped green chilies, set out in separate heaps. The fragrance of two limes quartered in a small steel bowl made my mouth water.

"Now," Kaki sat heavily on a chair, "you know what to do, yes or no? But most important, note proportions of ginger, garlic, kothimbir and chilies."

I squatted down, pulled out the heavy grinding stone from underneath the counter. I measured all the ingredients with my eyes, then laid them on the black stone. I moved the grinding pestle forwards and backwards, applied pressure with my arms until one spice was indistinguishable from the next. I moulded the wet paste into a round ball and placed it in a steel vati that Kamat Kaki held out to me. I took the vati from her and quickly ran my palms and fingers over its edge so as not to lose the pungent juices that covered my hands. I cleaned the grinding stone, slid it back under the counter.

Kaki removed the surmai from the fridge. Four thick cutlets of white fish lay in a shallow pool of brackish water, speckled yellow with tumeric. I drained the fish, then rubbed the newly ground masala into its firm body. Just as I was finishing, something twisted in my gut and I ran to the bathroom.

When I returned Kaki was beaming. "A little nausea doesn't hurt — it's a good sign," she said. I furrowed my forehead but she ignored my questioning glance. "Come back this evening, seven o'clock, yes or no. I'll fry surmai fresh for you then."

"I don't think so, Kaki. Not today. If just this much smell makes me sick then I don't think I'll survive the strong odour of frying fish. It's that coconut oil the cook used in the kadhi —"

"Do fish smells always send you running to the bathroom?" I shook my head. She looked at me shrewdly.

"No reason to worry then. I'll be waiting for you," she said, ushering me towards the front door, before I could protest.

This time the traffic intersection was not jammed. When I walked up to our flat, the front door was ajar. I could hear Kunda's tabalji adjusting the tablas to her high pitch. I left the door open for her music teacher.

I glanced at the clock on the way to the bathroom. It was quarter to eleven. I splashed water on my face, gargled a few times, lay down on Arvind's side of the bed. Looking at the restored boat which he had put on the night table that morning, I rubbed my ankles until the heaviness subsided. I reached across for his thermos; the outside of the steel tumbler turned cloudy as I poured some ice-cold water into it. After touching the tumbler to the centre parting of my hair, I put it to my mouth, my lips matching the imprint left by his mouth, and drank greedily, until the last drop was drained.

I propped up the pillows and leaned back. My eyelids began to gain weight. The wall clock ticked lazily . . . the second hand moved reluctantly . . . as though coming to a decision that this was a good time to end the journey, to prove to the world that infinity was maya, pure illusion . . . No more ticking, no more marching forward . . .

No more being afraid of that day when I will end up like Arvind's mother, tossing and turning in bed, window curtains tightly shut to mask the steady swing of the pendulum, seconds adding up to minutes, minutes adding up to hours . . . waiting, waiting for the sound of Arvind's car in the compound, the click of his hand on my doorknob. No more being afraid of the day when I will lose him, when he will remember the dimples, the hipster sari, the artfully arched eyebrows, the child-like smile, the snub nose, the long limbs that could have been his but are not. That one day he will regret all this, I know, because Kunda and I have found the answer to the question of why Arvind said yes to me. That is, I found the answer and when I told Kunda, she didn't refute my reasoning, merely said, with an uncharacteristic flash of maturity, "Stop thinking of Mona, Tara. She is far away in England and you are married to my brother because he chose you. Be content with that." I had looked at her, gratitude moistening my eyes; but something dark in me made me repeat: "He married me because unlike Mona, I'm plain and shy and he will never have to worry about any man paying attention to me, never worry that I will be disloyal."

If only the second hand would stop now, take a little rest from its relentless ticking, I wouldn't mind. As long as I could look at Arvind's framed photograph, glass reflecting clear sky, I shouldn't care. I would hold this moment: Kunda's thin, earnest voice stumbling on a complicated sequence of notes, the music teacher's true tones drowning her hesitation, showing her the way, the tabalji's hands on the tabla, heavy and slow. The silent crow on my windowsill, sharp beak searching black feathers. And Moti lying drowsily at my feet, too lazy to chase away the winged intruder. I wouldn't mind at all.

But if time stopped now, Manda wouldn't see, ever again, the ebbing and flowing of the sea from her window, tides dragged by the moon's journey around the earth, heaving surface pocked raw in the monsoon season, flushed pink with the setting sun. She wouldn't hear children's laughter from the adjoining building, wouldn't join in their game of hide and seek as they ran in and out of colourful curtains of drying clothes, wouldn't wave when they held up their toys for her to see.

If the second hand stopped now, Kunda wouldn't know the exquisite breathlessness caused by a large hand on the pale inside of her thigh, a wet tongue tracing the veins in the diaphanous tops of her ears . . .

And if time rested now, I would never feel Arvind's moist mouth against my neck, his massaging hands on the small of my back, the sweet pressure of his leg draping my hip.

The clock struck eleven.

I went to Manda's room and sat on the edge of her bed. She was listening to Vividh Bharati. I took her hands in mine. They were like butter, soft and pliable. "Want to play Scrabble?" I asked.

Manda nodded, singing along with the radio, her voice matching Lata's note for note, sweet, rich, mellifluous. When the song came to an end, she smiled at me.

I removed the game from the wardrobe, opened the lid and together we turned the letter bricks on their faces. When we were finished I picked seven, indicating to Manda that she do the same. She picked eight and instead of laying them on her letter bench, dropped them on the centre of the board and arranged them into a square, three letters to a side. She nudged into place the ones that were spilling over the lines. I took five of my own, added on another square, so that Manda's square and mine touched sides. We spent the next little while, earnest and giggling until the board was covered with square rooms. When all the bricks were used up, I lifted a brick from here and there so that some of the rooms now had doors and I was almost finished connecting each room to the other when Moti tipped the board with his paws. Manda and I fell back on the bed laughing. When I looked up, the professor was standing in the doorway.

I sat up in bed, smoothed down my sari and giving him a quick nod, ran to the kitchen to bring Manda's lunch to the dining table. The cook was making chapatis. Sakubai was filling the water jug.

"All plates are laid out," she sniffed. "Food also."

I heard the angelus from the Catholic convent from across the road. Twelve o'clock. It was later than I thought.

"Call them all to the table, then," I said to Sakubai and started serving the vegetables. Soon, everyone was seated.

"Are you finally going to eat with us?" Kunda asked me.

"Meaning what?"

"You've served yourself food. Ma has been telling you for months that you should eat with us, that Bai will serve the lunch. But now finally! You must be very hungry, Tara."

I thought for a moment. The queasy feeling was still there. Then I remembered Kaki's knowing nod, her beaming face: "A little nausea doesn't hurt. It's a good sign."

"Yes! I think I'm starving," I said, grinning at Kunda. She furrowed her forehead. I ignored her questioning glance and reaching across the table, helped myself to another chapati.

Our Family

The dead in our family never die. That's what Ajoba, Dad's
father, used to say when Anupama, Shirish, and I would cluster
around him, listening to stories about our ancestors, some of
whom we knew from various oil portraits that hung in our
house. It gave us a particular thrill to hear that at age ten our
great-grandfather — he of severe navy-blue handlebar mous-
taches and mahogany dragon-headed walking stick — had been
beaten with a rod by his father for pulverizing the lenses of a
brand-new pair of binoculars in order to obtain the ground glass
he needed to construct kite-strings; or, that Ajoba's sister had
rejected a prince in favour of a school teacher — a pauper even
by normal standards — because she had heard that his royal
highness's preferred hobby was killing mice that scrambled up
the river banks at twilight.

Ajoba would intersperse his stories with the refrain "The
dead in our family," and the three of us would complete it with
"never die."

At first, when he said "our family" I assumed he meant Mum's
side of the family too, but I was wrong. The realization came
one morning when Dad and I were visiting Mum's parents in
their two-storey house near Grant Road Station. I don't remember the purpose of that visit, but I do remember sitting on Dad's

lap, watching my grandfather eat his noonday meal at nine in the morning. As he slurped lentil curry, a tamarind moustache appeared on his upper lip and the conversation turned to resemblances. How Mum's dimpled chin was the exact replica of my grandmother's, how Anupama's "like-even-teeth-in-a-row" toes were exactly like Mum's, how Shirish's hairline was set way back on his forehead just like a first cousin's.

Before it was my turn to be compared, I said, "No, don't tell me who I look like. I'll tell you. I look like Dev Uncle. Dad showed me a photograph of Dev Uncle when he was my age. He looks just like me. Right, Dad?" I twisted my head in his direction. Dad nodded.

I turned and smiled at my grandfather who was glaring into his food, his jaw frozen mid-bite, his left hand reaching for a tumbler of water only to empty its contents onto his half-eaten plate. Dad's grip was tightening around my waist, my grandmother was prying me loose, leading me to the kitchen, stuffing dried fruit into my mouth. The sweetness of golden raisins mixed with the flavour of salty cashew nuts I will never forget.

I looked up. Dad was standing in the doorway, saying: "It's high time all of you got over him. Not one, not two, but twelve years since Dev passed away." He was shaking his head and my grandmother was shaking hers, too, and I wondered afterwards whether she was agreeing with Dad or regretting being unable to acknowledge her son's passing for fear the grief would overwhelm her. She took my clammy hand in hers and walked Dad and me to our car. I got in, picking at a scab on my elbow. When my grandmother lowered her face and smiled through the window, I averted my eyes and moved away. Her hand found my cheeks anyway, and caressing them she muttered, "Sweet, sweet Roopa. Sweeter than the sweetest jaggery ever eaten." I knew she was trying to console me but I pretended I didn't care, and twisting my elbow towards me, I lifted one end of my scab which was now hinging on its last leg. I peered inside: underneath lay an opaque lozenge of congealing blood.

"It's all your fault," I shouted at Dad when we'd passed Grant Road Station. "Why did you tell me I look like Dev Uncle? Why did you show me his photographs?"

"Because you do look like him and because I refuse to destroy photographs just because your uncle is dead. And since your grandfather is always so keen on having all three of my children resemble your mother's side of the family, he ought to have been pleased by what you said."

Dad was taking the longer route home, the one that goes by Worli sea-face. I looked out the window. Thick, scattered clouds gathered speed as they raced towards the shore. The hoarse, urgent coughing of horns, the elongated call of peanut hawkers, the swish of cars hurtling past, the heavy vibration from the Ambassador's engine under my feet: each exaggerated sound bounced off my ears separately.

"Don't worry about what happened this morning. Your mother, her family, they've had no practice with death. That's all," Dad said. His voice was calm. I turned towards him and the crescendo quality of the world petered away. He placed his left hand on my lap and I lay my right hand on his open palm. He squeezed my hand, repeating, "No practice with death, that's all."

I nodded. I knew what he meant: I was only twelve yet three relatives had died in our house since I was born.

Mashyakaka wasn't a permanent member of our household, but he would arrive every June for two months, a crate of mangoes in his arms, left cheek bulging with tobacco, fruit flies buzzing around his head. Anupama, Shirish, and I would let him drink his first cup of tea then zoom in with our questions: was it true that Nagpur became so hot in summer that pedestrians left footprints on the melting footpaths? Had he seen the bright orange on the newly painted Maruti temple when he'd gotten off at Dadar Station? Where was the snake fang he'd promised to bring? He would stuff a fresh slug of tobacco into his cheek then answer each of us; and sometimes I would lose the drift of his words, more enthralled by the deft way in which he settled and resettled the slimy wad in his mouth.

Then one June, when a moon-like sun was shining from behind a monsoon sky, Mashyakaka arrived as usual, the heavy buzz of fruit flies audible even before we opened the front door to greet him. The mango crate was laid on the floor and he was leaning against the wall; the corner of his mouth was wet with saliva. Aji shouted for Ramji to fetch a glass of water.

Early next morning, when Ramji entered Mashyakaka's room bearing a cup of tea, Mashyakaka was lying on the floor, his gold-rimmed pocket watch clutched to his chest. Ramji ran to fetch Aji. When she hurried to Mashyakaka's room — the rest of us following closely behind — she barely glanced at his crumpled body and turning her eyes ceiling-wards, said, "So! You finally decided to deliver him! Take away the cold tea, Ramji, for now he is drinking nectar of a different kind." Mashyakaka was our only relative who wore a farmer's turban and we remembered this and much else about him every time his name came up in conversation.

Ajoba was the next to go. His first heart attack was his last and he died at home before he could be removed to Nanavati Hospital. No sooner had we finished performing the religious rituals connected to his passing than Aji decided to go on a permanent fast. The doctor threatened to force-feed her and

Dad became so exasperated that he stopped going to her room when he returned from work every evening. But Aji knew what she was doing. She also knew that Dad couldn't keep away from her room forever. "No interest in food," she said to him the evening he broke his self-imposed exile. "It is not stubbornness what *you* call stubbornness. I haven't made up my mind *not* to eat. Simply don't feel like eating. And what do I have to live for? The better it will be for two of us the sooner I join your father."

Afterwards, whenever we remembered her, we didn't dwell on her shrinking frame nor the odour that had emanated from her mouth in putrid waves. Instead, we recalled her and Ajoba, in happier times.

Yes, I thought, tearing the scab from my elbow and flinging it out the car window, nobody can accuse our family — at least my father's side — of not having enough practice with death. The sea-face was behind us now. We would soon be home. I longed for Mum. Dad handed me his white handkerchief. "Wipe your face," he said. "You don't want your mother to see you upset, do you?"

Yes, I nodded, I do. But even though he wasn't looking my way, Dad had again read my mind. "Remember cremation-cremation?" he said, laying the handkerchief on my lap. I picked it up and rubbed my face.

Cremation-cremation was our favourite game. Or rather it used to be until Mum put a stop to it. Conceived by Anupama, our game went something like this: one of us would be the doctor (usually me), another the patient (normally Shirish), which left Anupama to play the role of the bungling compounder who would mix powders in such a way that the patient would die. The unlucky wretch would then have to be cremated. We were enacting this final scene of our drama when Mum walked in on us that last time we played the game. We had flattened Ajoba's collapsible armchair and Shirish was lying prone on it. Anupama and I had just finished stuffing old newspapers under him and she was reaching for a matchbox when Mum entered the verandah. Anupama didn't see her. She struck the match and was about to light the newspapers when Mum rushed forward and shoved her hand away.

"We're only pretending," Anupama said. I went and hugged Mum. She loosened my arms and bending down, sniffed under the armchair to make sure a hot flint hadn't lodged itself in the kindling we had prepared.

"See the water," Anupama said, pointing to a half-filled bucket at her side. "It's to put out the fire. Nothing would have happened."

"I told her, Mum," I said. "I told her not to use real matches. Ask Shirish if you don't believe me."

Mum turned to Shirish. His face was a sickly, puce-red: he played dead patient better than any of us. Mum shook him by the shoulders.

"He's only pretending," Anupama giggled, a slight shiver running through her voice. "And anyway, he's supposed to be dead."

When Shirish couldn't hold his breath any longer, he let out a snort and squirted laughter in Mum's face. "Fooled you," he said, sitting up. But when he saw her expression, he went behind her and put his arms around her waist. He'd started doing that recently. He was growing taller every month and his face now came up to Mum's neck. "I'm sorry," he said, twisting the end of her sari around his hand, motioning with his eyes that Anupama and I do the same and apologize. I did so, right away, but Anupama was defiant. Say sorry, Shirish glared at her, or else.

She had to mumble sorry then because she knew if she didn't, Shirish would send her to Coventry for a long time. Anupama liked to lead but didn't feel a leader unless Shirish was in the game. I didn't matter.

That night we stood outside the window that opens out on the verandah off my parents' bedroom and watched them argue.

"I cannot understand the morbid preoccupation with death that everyone in your family seems to have," Mum was saying.

"And I think it's very natural. Look at the location of our flat. Dead bodies have to pass Maya Building to get to the cremation grounds. The children see that, Leela. How can you or I expect to stop them from running to the balcony every time a funeral procession goes by? They're imaginative. They're only responding to what they see."

"That's exactly my point. What they're responding to is unhealthy. Not to mention dangerous. Matches! What will they think of next?" She shuddered.

"I will speak to them again but the point I'm trying to make is that one day, when you lose your reluctance to speak about death, the dead, you will see how very natural, in a way consoling —"

She turned away from Dad and addressed us at the window. "Don't any of you ever, ever, touch a match again. Do you understand? And don't forget: no playing together for a week. And Anupama, you don't play with the others for two weeks. Now close the verandah window and come in and say goodnight."

We closed the window and ran into their bedroom.

"Yes, yes, I know: that's why the dead in your family never die," Mum was saying.

Dad looked at her as he pulled the chair away from his writing table. "Coming to think of it, Leela, the same thing can be said of your family. But do you know why the dead in *your* family never die? Because the way all of you behave, it's as though they never lived." He started piling some papers that were strewn on top of his desk.

"Shirish, can you get a stool and close the window above the air conditioner?" Mum asked. Her voice was shaking. Dad turned and looked at her.

"There's a breeze," she said to him, her voice still not her own.

She complained frequently to anyone who did not live with us that she could smell burning flesh from the cremation grounds. When the wind picks up at night, the stench gets worse, she'd say.

Dad turned his back on us again and opened a file. "Goodnight," Mum said in our direction. Shirish stepped off the stool and started towards her, but she had already entered the bathroom.

"Come here," Dad said to us without turning around. "No more matches. Do you understand? No more matches. And don't let your mother catch you playing cremation-cremation again. Promise me." We nodded. He looked at Anupama. "How old are you?" he asked.

"Ten," she replied.

"And how old are Shirish and Roopa?"

"Nine and eight," she muttered.

"Well then, who is the oldest, the responsible one?"

Anupama had tears in her eyes. She ran out of the room. Shirish didn't try to talk to her that night and I followed his lead.

⌐

I was thinking about Ajoba and the story sessions we used to have when Nancy, Anupama's pen pal, visited us recently from

New Jersey. She was sitting at the dressing table one morning and I was combing out her long, blond hair.

"So, Siris will be coming for the wedding?" Nancy said.

"Who? Don't move. Please."

"Si-ris," she said, dividing the word so I could understand. She had figured out very quickly that even though we spoke English she didn't always understand us, nor we her. "When is he expected to arrive?"

"Who?" I said.

"Your brother. When is he arriving? For Anupama's wedding." Her tone showed a trace of irritation. I didn't blame her. Just two days in India, another three weeks to go. Her quest for understanding and being understood had just begun.

I looked at her in the mirror, removed the ribbon from my mouth. "He's dead," I said.

"Who?" It was her turn now.

"Shirish. My brother. He's dead." I finished tying the ribbon at the bottom of her plait and said, "You can move now." When she didn't, I looked at her face in the mirror. The scarlet patches on her cheeks and chin contrasted starkly with her blond hair. She wouldn't take her eyes off Anupama's lipstick stand on the dressing table.

"It's all right, Nancy," I said, sitting on the bed. "It's almost eight years ago that he died. Crossing the road. Hit by a car."

"But, last night," she said, shaking her head, "while we were eating dinner. You were talking about him as if he were alive."

"No, we weren't."

"Yes, you were. You know, when all of you were discussing the oil painting Anupama's artist friend gave her as a wedding gift?"

Yes, I nodded.

"Anupama said that the boy in the painting looked just like Siris. She said she considers it a lucky sign, or something."

I looked at her blankly, still trying to remember when anybody had said anything to make Shirish alive. There had been ten of us last night. It was a buffet. I remembered the painting, of course. It was modern, with triangles, circles, rectangles, red, yellow, purple, and green. And in the upper right-hand corner the face of a boy, the one who reminded Anupama of Shirish.

"Don't you remember?" Nancy said, "I asked you who Siris was and you said, 'My brother.'"

"Ah . . . Of course, I remember, Nancy. I'm sorry. Then you said that Anupama hadn't written to you about any brother and I said, 'Hadn't she?' And *you* said, 'That's very odd because we exchanged details about our families in our very first letters to each other.'"

"Exactly. And you replied, 'Oh, Anupama must have forgotten to tell you about him,'" Nancy said, getting convinced by the minute that she had been fully justified in believing Shirish to be alive. And I was beginning to think so too because I now remembered telling everyone about the dream I'd had, of Shirish coming for Anupama's wedding, dressed in an embroidered sherwani and presenting her with complete plans for her new bungalow. And Dad had remarked that if anyone was capable of building a bungalow to suit Anupama's specifications, it would be Shirish. Or something to that effect.

I smiled at Nancy. "Where did you think he was coming from? For the wedding, I mean."

"So many of your cousins are studying abroad. I assumed he was too. Doing engineering or architecture, or something —"

"Poor Nancy," I said.

"I kept wondering why Anupama hadn't told me about him. And never once did I suspect the truth. Even your mother spoke as though —"

"What do you mean? I don't remember Mum being in the room when the painting was discussed. She wasn't there afterwards either, when I told my dream."

"Well then, she must have overheard us," Nancy said.

I was starting to get off the bed but sat down again. It was my turn to use the bathroom next. Anupama had stopped splashing in there. She opened the door and came out.

"Nancy didn't know about Shirish," I said to her. "She said the way we were talking about him last night, she thought he was doing post-graduate work abroad."

"Oh?" Anupama said, removing the towel from her hair.

"It must be wonderful to remember him as though he were still alive," Nancy said. "I mean —"

"But, listen to this, Anupama," I interrupted. "Mum spoke about Shirish. To her. Tell us what she said, Nancy."

"Well, I went to your parents' bedroom to choose the sari I'm going to wear to the wedding —"

"Yes, yes, but what did Mum say about Shirish?" Anupama asked. I knew it still rankled her that we couldn't talk about him when Mum was around.

"I'm trying to tell you as fast as I can."

"Sorry," I said, "go on."

"Your Mum said she has been dreaming about Siris too. She told me her dream: All of you are gathered in your living room after the wedding reception. Everything has gone off well and now only the sad part remains, the part where she has to say good-bye to you, Anupama. She hugs you at the door, turns around, and goes onto the front balcony. Siris is there. He smiles, goes behind her and puts his arms around her waist. That's all she told me."

I glanced sideways at Anupama. She had been standing very still when Nancy was talking. She bent over quickly now and rubbed her newly washed hair with her towel. She stayed bent for a long time. When she straightened up, her face was flushed and her eyes had a scrubbed, shiny look. And as I got off the bed, Ajoba's refrain, which had lain dormant in my mind since Shirish's death, came back to life.

Shantabai

From Bombay they catch a train to Poona. The air is cooler now. The half-empty bogie smells of Brahmi hair oil and ripe mangoes. In order to catch the earliest train, they left without bathing and because they were the first to board the compartment, they each have a window seat. Shantabai — Nalutai Wadkar's maidservant — and Veena — Nalutai's twenty-year-old daughter.

Unlike Veena, who sits so still, face emptied of expression, Shantabai has a complete sense of who she is this morning: an Adivasi of the Warli Tribe, most recently the Wadkar cook, now surrogate mother to Veena. And unlike Veena, who wears a crumpled, overnight churidaar, Shantabai is dressed in a starched, pink, nine-yard sari, a two-by-two red blouse matching its thin, contrasting border. No more servants sniggering at my vanity, she thinks, arranging the folds on her lap, no more cooks jealous of my keeping up with the memsahibs. She touches the banana pouch at her waist; the hardness of the gold ingot is comforting. She hunches her shoulders; the roll of rupee notes Nalutai thrust into her hand this morning pokes the valley between her breasts. She leans forward, pats Veena's knee. Veena closes her eyes. Sleep, Shantabai thinks, be lulled by the rocking of the train. From now on your sorrow will be my sorrow, my caresses your balm. If only I could tell you, Veena, how much I longed to do things for you, beginning with the mornings when I stood at your mother's bedside, cradling your whimpering face against my shoulder, resisting an urge to put you to my breast, because you were hungry and your Ma always nursed your twin sister, Sarla, first. If only I could tell you how I would pretend you were mine afterwards, when I trickled milk into your mouth one silver teaspoon at a time, sang you stories about my pada.

Shanta is crawling in the earth-swept front yard, her dark skin the colour of the gnarled, skeleton-like tree trunks that hold up her family dwelling. Her small, loosely clutched fists brush spikes of brown grass as she moves along, eyes trained on the earth directly under her gaze, heedless of a colony of black ants building themselves into pyramids only a foot away.

It will not be long before Shanta will be able to crush those ants, frighten their beings, send them scurrying in fifty directions. Yet it is unlikely that maiming and terrorizing will hold any interest for her, because she will never have seen her older brother, Dashmya, do this. He does not use the stick which is always attached to some part of his body — tucked into his striped, knee-length underpants, into the black string he wears around his wrist — except to run it along the wooden spikes designed to keep the neighbours' goats out of the yard.

Dashmya has erected this fence himself, first carrying the twigs from the forest, whittling them into even length and shape, removing the rocks from the area to be staked. The dislodged rocks are piled in the backyard, securely stacked so they will not topple over and injure his baby of a sister, who touches, smells, samples, grabs, fearless, innocent, free.

Three years later, when Shanta is climbing this heap, Dashmya will keep a close watch on her, cup her rounded heels in his palms, wedge his roughened hands between her knees and the jagged rocks as she slides backwards. And when Shanta is five, she will follow him everywhere except into the jungle, where he will refuse to take her. "One day, when you are as high as gate, yes. I will show you footprints of deer, wild wolves, and even wilder hyenas, point out paths they have created with their bodies, flowers they have sniffed along the way." His words will not come out like that but Shanta will understand the garbled, tumbling sentences, the accompanying movement of his hands, the rolling of his eyes and head, the squiggles he makes with his toes. And to soften his emphatic refusal, he will stop whittling a piece of white wood, take her on his lap, measure her palms against his, uncurl her small, rounded fingers, stretch his own. She will giggle then, her universe filled by his presence, by her Dashmya who sometimes slings her on his shoulders like a gunny sack. She will not mind that the backs of his hands and fingers are streaked with the saliva he wipes from the corners of his mouth, not mind the thick crust she will remove from the inside of his eyes. It is this face, this sour smell of his hands, this constant presence in the corner of the yard, this stringy feel of his arms when he holds her up so that she is his sky and he is her earth, it is all this she will remember when years later he will disappear into the jungle, never to return.

People from a nearby construction site are running alongside the train, pointing, grinning, shouting, tripping over stones and stumps of tree trunks covered in shoots and golden spikes of grass. Slowly, in increasing jerks, the train comes to a halt. Nobody from the ladies' compartment disembarks. Shantabai walks down the bogie to the compartment door, lifts the window, and, ducking her shoulders, pokes her head out. There's a cluster of people at the front of the train, the ones at the back of the knot craning their necks forward to get a better view. She looks the other way. An old man is gazing at her, wrinkled thighs thin like his arms, a loin cloth not fully covering shriv-elled, drooping parts. A threadbare cotton pancha is draped around his neck; on his head a dusty yellow turban. He finishes chewing his tobacco, then spits it in a thin red stream that hits the ground six feet away. "Bullock cart on railway track," he says, in a voice husky and filled with strong, leaf-rolled bidis.

"How did it get there?" Shantabai asks, scanning the hilly terrain. No fields, no cultivation in sight. The old man doesn't answer, just shakes his head slowly, which Shantabai interprets to mean, if I had answers to all the whys, hows, whats, and whens, I wouldn't be here now, would I?

"Is anyone dead?" she asks.

The old man shakes his head vigorously, then says, "Only bullock."

"Bullock cart on rail track. No one dead!" Shantabai announces, pulling her head back in. "Get out and look for yourselves," she tells the women crowding behind her. She weaves her way back to Veena who has heard what the old man said.

"Look, Shantabai. Vultures. The bullock must have been dead on the track quite a while before our train got here." Veena is peering at the sky. Shantabai shudders at the large birds hovering above, screeching, circling, skimming the earth in impatient loops. "They don't want us. They resent our presence," Veena mutters to herself, her lips twisting. Shantabai glances at the textbook Veena is holding, and seeing a letter, recognizes Baba Saheb's handwriting immediately. Veena quickly closes the book.

"When did you get that letter? He shouldn't be writing to you — it is being no good, Veena. What happened with your sister's husband, Baba Saheb, happened. What is *going* to happen only you can control." Veena is massaging the sides of her neck. She ruffles her book and finding the page she is looking for, holds it up in front of her face, but not before Shantabai has seen her expression, which is animated, almost optimistic. Shantabai leans back against the seat, covers her mouth with the end of her sari.

"Look at clean sky above you!" The man in the white, khadi pyjama-kurta is shouting into a megaphone. Shanta wishes he wouldn't be so loud. His distorted voice punctures the inner walls of her head like a sharp rock. Besides, he doesn't need the large funnel-shaped thing; there are exactly six villagers at his feet, two of whom are dozing, heads lolling against the banyan tree. "Look up!" the khadi man thunders. "Why do dark clouds that used to gather above the village gather no more? Why river is shrivelled down to jagged stones? Why grass has forgotten its taste of dew?" The khadi man is punching the air with his fists.

A villager who is leaning against the tree trunk gives a loud snort and opening one eye says, "Are we honoured to have amongst us poet or politician?"

But the khadi man does not hear, so lost is he in the echo of his own voice, so mesmerized by the quality of his rhetoric. "Look around you: there is no planting, no plucking, no ploughing. Drought was predicted months ago by wise men amongst you, men who interpret sky and smell of earth better than astrologers read movement of stars. But did government listen? No! Instead of giving you water supply, they gave it to baday-baday landlords who want irrigation canals to lead directly to their private fields, whose badmaash sons do dadagiri in water-user associations, who have big-big influence on Congress-I Government. This will not happen if you vote Janata. We will bring water to your doorstep, negotiate top-top wages at harvest time!"

Shanta looks down the road. The village is a rusty red; trees, shrubs, mud huts coated in fine dust that swirls everywhere. Somewhere, a child starts to cry, his rasping poignant after the gilded promises of the khadi man. There must be grit on the soft insides of his pink, baby eyelids, Shanta thinks, grit lining his throat. But there is no stopping the dry gusts that bleed in through doors and windows causing hut-insides to take on the colour of the landscape.

Shanta hasn't seen Dashmya since sunrise, not since he gave her some grass to suck on then disappeared into the jungle. Let him find different roots and berries, she prays, the same ones again and my stomach will turn inside

135

out. She looks at the khadi man who is getting into his jeep. She wishes she could bring him to meet Ba, her grandmother, take him to their bare, odourless kitchen, show him a tightly furled heap which once used to be her strong, lean body. "The village is paying for the loggers' sins!" Ba will tell the khadi man, her voice weak, then rising, coarse, "The village is paying for you politicians' sins. Countless times have I not said government's unwillingness to prevent chopping trees is at bottom of all our troubles. No trees, no rain. Do you know how many flowering trees our jungle used to have? Three hundred! And do you know why there were so many? Listen and I will tell you. Imagine jungle is our pada; the trees are its people. A tree from Paru Gully marries a tree from Shevanti Gully, a tree from Bada Naka marries a tree from Chota Naka. So when new trees are born, they take on good of both parents. Young Paru-Shevanti will be narrow-trunked like the trees of Paru Gully, sturdy like the trees of Shevanti Gully. The Bada-Chota will be tall and strong like trees of Bada Naka, slender and resilient like those of Chota Naka. They will then survive drenching monsoons, severe droughts, flooding rains. Even the smallest child in pada knows," Ba will scorn the khadi man, "that jungle is like a person: breathing, living, thinking, capable of dying if not allowed to look after itself."

But the fourteen-year-old Shanta closes her eyes against the dust raised by the disappearing Jeep, wishing for a moment she could sit on its roof, ride all the way to the city, ride into a future of cement houses, hungerless days, clean, uncreased rupee notes like the wads the moneylender keeps locked inside his desk.

She walks back to their hut, enters the kitchen, shaking her head at the evil star of drought that is fixed above their village. Looking down at Ba, she remembers twilights when, after lighting the lamp in front of Lord Shiva and praying that Bad Luck may never turn their way, Ba would relate to her and Dashmya instances when people of the village had willed harm on one another, sometimes for imagined wrongs, other times for real grievances. Dashmya would shake his head then cover his hands over his ears. He didn't want to hear about the contorted, treacherous path a human mind could take.

He wanted to know where certain plants could be found; and armed with this information he would go in search every morning, return home exhausted, carrying a sack full of roots and herbs and berries which Ba would then pound and compound into medicinal packets.

But it will not be until a year later, when Shanta is fifteen, that she will fully realize that Dashmya's shivering in their father's presence, his doltish unwillingness to accompany the rest of the villagers to earn a day's living, his garbled, convoluted answers, were deliberately exaggerated in order to prevent any outsider from entering his world. She will think all these thoughts as she waits for Dashmya to come out of the jungle, resignation, anger, hope, despair shaping her dreams as days become months become years.

The ripe mango smell is gone. Shantabai opens her eyes. The train is moving now. She looks down; there are two bananas on her lap. She raises her eyebrows at Veena who tips her head sideways. Sitting on the other side of the compartment is a woman with a basket of fruit on her lap. The phalwali, sensing the gaze she is under, turns her face away from the window, looks at Shantabai. "Tell Tai to eat," she whispers loudly, sticking out her elbow Veena's way. "Simply crying all the time. Is mother, father dead? I gave bananas. She didn't want so I put them on your lap — tell her to eat. Little food will do good. Simply crying all the time." She clicks her tongue, gives Shantabai a sympathetic but encouraging look as though she is sure that Shantabai will do the necessary: make Tai eat.

Veena is wiping her streaked face with her dupatta; her textbook is fluttering on the seat; Baba Saheb's letter has been put away. "Not to worry, Veena," Shantabai says, softly, "your father has arranged everything. He personally spoke to cook in Poona guest house. Lallusing, cook's name is, will meet us at Shivaji Nagar. You concentrate on your studies. Not long before your final exams when I will take you back to Bombay.

Wadkar Saheb said I'm to stay with you in Ganesh Lodge this time. Afterwards, after exams, we'll come back to Poona. M.A. Shem-A, whatever you want, you can do in Poona. I told your father I'll be not moving to Vizak with your mother. I will stay with you."

Veena's face is wet again. "Don't ever leave me, Shantabai, don't ever leave me."

Shantabai is holding out a banana, its peeled skin drooping like wilting petals. Veena shakes her head. Shantabai lays it on the seat and leaning across, rubs Veena's cheeks with her palms. "Don't talk like that, Veena. I'll not be leaving you. Everything will work out. You'll see. Did you speak to your Ma after your Papa called from Vizak last night?" Shantabai takes a bite of the banana.

"Why would I speak to Ma! You know I haven't. She threw me out of the house, remember! I don't want to speak to her ever again — besides, Sarla may answer the phone." Veena reaches back and pulls her plait in front. Her fingers stroke its length; the top of her plait from which the mogra garland used to hang feels empty. She stands up, eyes filling again, and without looking at Shantabai, walks down the bogie towards the rear of the compartment. Shantabai lets the tears she is holding back trickle down her throat.

It is afternoon now, and the sun is more fierce than the noonday sun. The drought is in its second year. Shanta paws the scorched earth with her feet. She walks to the end of the village. The black highway snakes in the distance, imaginary water shining in every dip and crease. She saunters back to their mud hut, her eyes scanning tinder-dry roofs under which crumpled, angled bodies must doze in dehydrated stupor. She lies beneath the banyan tree in their front yard, stretches her arms upwards to catch its dry, hanging roots; they are too far away.

She thinks of Dashmya, out in the jungle, looking for the last of the moisture-filled leaves. It won't be long before he will be back, she knows, holding out a wilting bunch, head hanging in shame because he was unable to prevent their father last night. Even though one part of her wants to tell Dashmya that she is grateful for the fight he put up for her, another part does not want to see him. Not him, nor anybody else. See nothing, feel nothing, hear nothing. But try as she will the sounds of Dashmya and her father wrestling in the darkened threshold of her room surround every thought. She works her mouth, turns her head, spits into the dry ground. As if out of nowhere ants swarm over its shining wetness.

For six months now the chickoo trees have scratched the sky with bare arms. Six months that her father has had no fruit to pick, six months that he has drowned himself in tadi, his once wiry body now emaciated, thick lips prominent in thin, creased face. Eight months since her grandmother passed away, her shrunken body like a ten-year-old's on the funeral pyre.

"Where was your spirit last night, Ba, the one you promised would look after me after you were gone?" Shanta shouts. Her words stick in her throat as if in the midst of a bad dream. "Why weren't you there Ba, guarding with Dashmya my threshold last night? I should have known something was wrong when he put forefinger to lips. Ssshh. But so exhausted was I with hunger I couldn't keep my eyes open. The next thing I knew, he and Father were fighting, clawing, rolling . . . Then Father is snatching stick from Dashmya, a sharp crack, like coconut dashed against a rock and Dashmya's body a crumpled heap in my doorway. And even as I sensed old man's breath on my stomach, and even before I smelled his filthy smell, and felt the bottomless pain, I had my first encounter with Living Death. If only I had drowned on the vile sourness that rose up in my throat. But where is Dashmya now? Lead me to him, Ba. Or else bring him home."

Shantabai and Veena pull back involuntarily as a train rushes along parallel tracks, streaks past in the opposite direction. Neither of them have said a word to each other for over half an hour.

Outside, the country is in dusty bloom. Inside, a thin woman with a well-oiled bun sitting on top of her head opens a tiffin carrier. The slightly fermented, appetizing smell of curds and rice fills the compartment; she unfolds a small packet of hot lime pickle. Shantabai cannot drag her eyes off the food. Her stomach rumbles even though it isn't long since she ate the two bananas. She fervently prays that Lallusing or whatever cook's name is has prepared a big lunch. She smiles at the eating woman when her protesting stomach makes itself heard. The woman says, "Can you believe I used two vatis of curds for this much rice. See how rice has absorbed it all! Every time I am telling myself put more curd put more curd but when I am mixing it at home it looks too wet, like a kadhi. Then when I'm opening tiffin four hours later all curd is gone, rice has eaten it!" The woman beams at Shantabai, her strong jaws masticating the bloated grains, her darting tongue licking the lime pickle from the corner of her mouth. "You should have bought something to eat at Lonavla Station," she smiles at Shantabai. "Peanut-cashew chikki, something. Also garam tea."

"We'll be in Poona soon," Shantabai says. "Not much longer I don't think." She watches the woman finish her meal.

"Will you keep eye on my things?" the woman asks Shantabai, walking towards the toilet with her tiffin carrier, presumably to rinse it. Shantabai nods.

"How is Sarla?" Veena's soft question catches Shantabai unawares.

"Mourning," she answers, her eyes drawn to a crooked queue of stationary motor cars waiting at a gateless railway crossing. Veena flinches, runs her fingers along the lining of the window, moves back when a cloud of dust is released into the air. "Six days ago everything normal," Shantabai sighs, "then trrr-phat, everything is broken. That look on your mother's face when she dragged you to door, threw you out, I will never forget. Ever since you left, Veena, Sarla is simply sitting in her room, on top of bed, exam books open in front. Crying, crying. Why don't you talk to her? Write her letter from Poona. Say how sorry you are, that you and Baba Saheb did what you did in weak moment. We are all worried about baby. Think about your unborn nephew, write her letter —"

"I can't, Shantabai, don't you see? She will never forgive me. Her own twin sister with her own husband. I know her torture, Shantabai. Don't you know my mind is also filled of visions of how they must be together —"

"Toba, Veena, toba!" Shantabai smacks her own face with her left hand, first one cheek then the other. "You have no right to imagine your sister and her husband. You must forget him, you must. To him you were simply there, so he did shameful thing that he did. You don't know men, Veena, you don't know men."

"Baba is different, Shantabai. Why can't anyone understand that? He will stand by me —"

"And what about his wife? Think, Veena: your own sister and her unborn child. He won't be leaving her. Are you listening to me?"

"He will stand by me. You heard him, Shantabai, the way he kept pleading with Ma not to throw me out. But Ma didn't listen. Never does."

"He just said that because he didn't want to see you thrown out on street —"

"Ha! My point exactly. He cares for me. And he came with me, didn't he, when Ma threw me out, took me to Ganesh Lodge. Didn't go back to Sarla that night, did he? He loves both of us, Shantabai, don't you understand? He loves us both."

"What are you saying, Veena? That he'll marry you as well? Talk sense. Forget him. Get M.A. Shem-A. Your father will find

you good boy in Poona. Nobody knows what happened between you and Baba Saheb. Your Ma is telling everyone that
you got high fever and because Sarla is at home, pregnant, too
much risk for unborn baby. Where are you going, Veena?"

"What do you think? To jump out of the train so everyone will be rid of me. Sit down, Shantabai, I'm going to the
bathroom."

*By morning the Vanzari's odour — dense, matted hair, greasy bedding,
earth-choked fingernails — straddles Shanta's village from side to side.
Only a handful of villagers smell the accompanying aroma of lemon grass,
incense, camphor-oil. At midday, the village headman goes out to meet the
Vanzari strangers, sternly reminds them of the last time they pitched tents
on the other side of the river. Cooking utensils, drying garments, nobs of
coal, headkerchiefs had disappeared overnight. "If you do not leave by
tonight," Shanta's headman warns, "I cannot vouch for tomorrow."*

*The King of the Vanzari scans the headman as though scouting the
horizon. He notices his flimsy thighs, hollow belly, turban reduced to a
transparent thinness. The Vanzari Raja does not say that this is the first
time he and his people have wandered this far south. Says nothing of their
unwritten, unbroken code: never to take anything from anybody who has
nothing to give. He nods his head, walks backward to his people standing
in a cordon behind him.*

*That night, as Shanta approaches the river, the gurgling, bubbling
sounds of countless vessels being filled, refilled, draws her onwards. The
Vanzaris are bathing silently, mesmerized by the clean coolness of the water.
They throw trusting infants high above their heads, embrace them midair,
hold them underwater until their bodies squirm and wriggle like little eels.
And from downriver, in the highest of singing voices float ancient chants,
resonant of the equinox, the changing seasons, ingathering, fruitage. Shanta
runs out from behind the palm tree, sari held high above her ankles, impatient
to shout out in the pada: "The strangers smell because they come from a place*

142

where there is no water. Come look at them now! How clean they are —"

Then there he is, blocking her path, standing arms akimbo: a Vanzari youth. Water drips over his lean torso, fills white loincloth, trickles down slender thighs, darkening the soft earth underneath his feet. Shanta drops her eyes as he walks towards her. He takes her hand, leads her away from the river and lies down on his back, at the edge of the jungle. Shanta sits next to him, looking at the wispy treetops that brush the moonlit sky. How many months have I waited here, she wonders, since that night Dashmya disappeared. First, I waited for him, then, as the weeks became months became years, I waited for his spirit. How much longer must I wait for your spirit Dashmya, she whispers aloud, forgetting for a moment the boy who is lying on the earth beside her.

"The river is dying," the Vanzari youth is saying.

Shanta shakes her head. "Not any more. This year we had monsoon rains. You should have seen river before. It was barely a trickle then."

The boy is stubborn and confident, Shanta can tell by the expression in his eyes. "Your river is dying. The Vanzari know. My people are nomads and we see everything. Fifty miles farther up, on other side of jungle, they have diverted the water. Your village will have to move someday. Tell your headman that. Your people can go to city — enough work there to fill many bellies. You speak to your mother, your father — What's the matter? Are you cold?" Shanta doesn't move when he kneads her soles, doesn't flinch when his warm hands travel upward, caress her thighs; a restless stirring urges her to open them wider. Afterwards, when she wakes up, he is gone. Looking down, she sees something glinting on her chest. It is the gold ingot that had hung around the Vanzari's neck, the gold ingot which is now reflecting a harvest moon.

Someone is waving out to them as they disembark from the train at Shivaji Nagar. Someone who looks what a Lallusing would look like, Shantabai thinks: short, sturdy legs, a cook's rounded belly, a little tufted shendi sprouting from the back of his shaven scalp. She nods at him. He comes forward with joined hands, bows his head slightly in Veena's direction.

"Saheb rang from Vizak," he says, grinning. "Told me Veena Didi is not well." His expression takes on an appropriate somreness, a hang-dog look.

"Don't just stand there," Shantabai says. "Take bags from Veena Didi's hands!"

"I told Vizak Saheb not to worry," Lallusing continues, not even glancing in Shantabai's direction. "I will look after her, I said, and phataphat, Didi will be well, smiling. You look tired, Didi. Let me take your handbags. Ricksha is waiting outside. Come, come. Nashta is all ready at guest house."

Ignoring the large suitcase at Shantabai's feet, he takes the three bags out of Veena's hands, starts walking towards the exit. Veena smiles at Shantabai and together they lift the suitcase, follow Lallusing outside.

"Whyfor Didi did you carry heavy-heavy luggage?" Lallusing says. "Give it to me and I'll load it for you. I came on cycle, so you go ahead. Rickshawalla, straight to Prabhat Road, phataphat. The mali is there, Didi, he will let you in."

Shantabai is pleased that Veena is smiling.

The mali is watering a row of white lilies. He lets them into the house. After he has carried their belongings upstairs, he enters the sitting room.

"There was phone call for Veena Didi," he says.

"Must have been your father from Vizak," Shantabai says.

"No, no. Not Vizak Saheb," the mali asserts. "Phone call is coming from Bombay."

"Must have been your mother," Shantabai says.

"No, no. A man, from Bombay, asking if Veena Didi had arrived."

"Did he say anything? Any message?" Veena's voice is soft.

"No. Only that he will call back." The mali turns to Shantabai. "Lallusing will be here soon but Didi must be hungry. I'll show you where kitchen is."

As Shantabai follows the mali, she sees Veena insert two lilies she plucked earlier, into the top of her plait.

Clutching the ingot in her right hand, Shanta walks to the path that leads into the jungle. Hearing a rustle, she takes two steps in. The jungle floor is dappled. Shining eyes fade as a deer retreats into night shadows. Shanta crouches and breaks off a wild flower, its colour masked by darkness. Holding it in her left hand, she returns to the village. Da-sh-mya, not com-ing back, Da-sh-mya, not com-ing back: the uncoiling river, the chirruping grasshoppers, the unopened flowers, the unbroken sky, she hears them all whisper.

Shanta does not know it yet, but this realization will take her to the city, away from her people, her pada, her father, never to return. But she will leave while the river is flowing, the jungle is standing tall, the villagers are picking rich men's fruit.

And it will not be until much later, long after she has begun working for the Wadkars in Bombay, that Sarla, the sociology student, twin sister of Veena, will read aloud from her textbook details about Shantabai's Adivasi pada, tell her about the mixed dialect spoken by her people. And it will be at this time that Shantabai will learn that Adivasi means Bhoomiputra means "original people of the land" and she will know why Ba would refer to the jungle as their neighbouring village, the trees as their kinsmen. And it is at this time that she will fully understand why it was so appropriate that Dashmya choose the lap of the jungle to seek his solace.

And it will not be until Shantabai is taking care of Veena in Poona that she will learn that life simply happens, that even a soft-boned, well-meaning sister can wound her beloved twin through no willed fault of her own. That a man can stand by his mistake, give up a promising career by openly keeping two women because he honours them both, because he takes responsibility, accepts consequences. And when Veena and Sarla will continue to live in Poona and Bombay, never communicating with each other except through a deep-seated instinct which tells them how profoundly the other is suffering, Shantabai will understand that even though it is impossible to forget, it is not always impossible to forgive.

Sensible About Matters of Heart

⁓

I

The public announcement system jangled overhead. The flight number, which I barely discerned through tinny static, was not mine. Less than a week in India and I was already back at the airport, this time catching a domestic flight to Madras.

"Did you check the dining table before leaving the flat, Shaila?" Mum asked. "Bayabai left the ladoos to cool under the fan."

"Yes, Mum, yes," I replied. "You've already asked me that!"

"This irritability must stop. You need to forget what happened between you and Simon. You'll see," she continued, her voice softening, "Mina and Ravi's wedding in Madras will be the perfect opportunity to do that."

"Maybe it will," I shrugged, "but I wish you hadn't promised Mina I would go for her wedding without asking me first. Not only that, you even went and booked my plane ticket. Now I have no choice." I looked out the window; someone had cleaned the glass with a wet, dirty cloth.

My flight was announced.

"Here Shailu," Mum said, thrusting into my hands her gold chain with the ivory Ganapati locket my grandmother had given her when she'd married Dad. "It'll help you in your state of mind."

I closed my fist around the locket and slipped it into the change compartment of my wallet. I smiled and hugged her quickly. "I'll see you day after tomorrow," I said. Her fresh shikeykai smell stayed with me until I boarded the plane. I sat down and looked out the window. The thick, weather-resistant double panes made the tarmac appear farther away than it was.

In August 1972, Simon fell out of love with me and in love with Jenny. I saw them one midnight, arms linked, crossing the road in Osborne Village. It was a clear Winnipeg night, the sky arching overhead like an inky dome. I was on my way home after doing a locum at St. Boniface Hospital, wondering whether or not Simon had decided between Vancouver and Calgary. I had job offers in both places.

Jenny was wearing a checked madras shirt, a leather thong tied around her forehead, fastened in a knot against her golden hair. They were so absorbed in each other they didn't notice my car, only second at the traffic lights.

I phoned Simon the minute I got home; nobody answered. The next morning he phoned me and said he had called me the previous night to join him and a bunch of people —

"I'm doing a locum, remember?" I cut in.

"How was I to know you were on call? Is anything the matter?"

"Was Jenny there?"

"Yes. I walked her home afterwards."

"I'll see you whenever I see you, Simon," I said. "Life is busy at the hospital these days."

I put the phone down before he could protest. He had told me there was nothing going on between him and Jenny; I didn't believe him.

The phone rang again. "Don't do this to yourself," Simon said. "There is nothing between Jenny and me. She doesn't even live here."

"Where does she live?"

"With her mother, somewhere in Ontario. Her parents are divorced. She's just here visiting her dad." Her father, I already knew, was dean of medicine. "Come on Shaila, this is ridiculous."

"Okay," I said, giving in. "Will I see you tonight?"

"Come over after you finish at the hospital," he said.

Simon had been waiting for me at the airport the night I returned from my trip home for Dad's sixtieth birthday. I was so relieved to see him that I threw my arms around his neck.

"I suppose this means you'll marry me," he had said into my hair. It was the first time we had embraced in public.

"Yes. Yes. Yes," I had said, not wanting to let go of him.

I stepped out of the plane at Madras and the heat from the shimmering tarmac rushed up to meet my face. I walked into the terminal building. The air conditioning inside made me shiver.

"I thought Canada would have toughened you up!" I turned, gave Anil a lopsided smile. I hadn't seen him for nine years. He smiled back and said, "Give me your baggage tags. Wait for me under that tourist poster, the one of Mahabalipuram."

It had been a long time since anyone had told me what to do. Anil came from a world where men followed one set of rules, women another. A world where adulthood was a boundary beyond which girls lost their identities, became suitable wives.

Despite our differences, whenever Anil and I saw each other we were irresistibly drawn together; it was pure chemistry. The last time we met was in Mina's hostel room, before he left for Calcutta. He had finished his commerce degree, and I was in first-year medicine. Outside, sea breezes rustled leaning palms;

149

inside, the ceiling fan whirred lazily, twenty tk-tk-tks to a minute. Limescented aftershave mingled with Rexona soap and a haze of finality, of feverishness hung over our rendezvous. Tracing the veins on my throat with his fingertips, Anil said, "I don't want to screw things up for you, Shaila, you know, with your husband, after you're married. So we won't go all the way. All right?" I thought him arrogant, but nodded agreement.

Later on, just before jumping out of the ground-floor window, he said, "I'll tell you something, Shaila. One day, no matter how old we are — who knows, we may even be married — we'll meet again and then, believe me, we will come together."

Anil came towards me now, carrying both my suitcases. I followed him out the terminal to a black Fiat. "I borrowed Ravi's car," he said, placing my cases in the trunk. "I met him when we were both studying at the Indian Institute of Management in Calcutta. Small world, isn't it?"

"Where am I staying?" I asked. "Mina said to just come, that she'd take care of everything else."

"Well, Mina and her family are staying at Ravi's company guest house. Ravi's house is overflowing with relatives, so all of us, you, me, and the rest of his Calcutta I.I.M. friends and Mina's Bangalore friends, are being put up at Woodlands Hotel."

"We are?" I suddenly wasn't sure about this arrangement. I guessed Anil wasn't married because I felt certain that whatever information Mina had withheld, she would have told me this. I wondered if she was trying to matchmake. She didn't know about Simon. And now there was nothing to tell.

In September, after Simon and I decided on Calgary, we took a week off and drove west to the Rockies. The sky seemed to move with us, sweeping forward.

We stopped in Banff and it was everything I wanted it to be.

Wispy clouds feathering a blue sky, a canoe gliding beneath Victoria Glacier, huge elk moving in waves of brown and grey along the mountainside. We decided to stay the night.

"What say you we give Sulphur Mountains a miss?" Simon said. "You don't want to go to —"

"Those smelly hot springs?" I laughed. "You must be joking."

"In that case," he muttered, leaning against my shoulders until my elbows gave way and I was flat on my back.

I rolled up my car window as Anil pulled into the parking lot of Woodlands Hotel. "I haven't had lunch yet," he said. "Want to join me?"

I nodded. I was starving.

Woodlands Restaurant smelled as though I had stepped into the dining room of the gods. Hot, spiced, fragrant sambar, pungent green coconut chutney, the sourish scent of idli and dosa mingled enticingly in tinkling air. I ordered one plate of paper dosa with potato bhaji and another of idli-sambar.

Just as I was dipping feather light idli into steaming sambar, Anil said, "I'm engaged."

Black spots flickered in front of my eyes; I put down my spoon carefully. The idli floated, a white island amid a fragrant curry of onions and potatoes.

He gently nudged my foot under the table. "I had to tell you!" he said, motioning to a waiter to bring me water.

"Can't drink water. Not back long enough for my immune system to have kicked in," I said. "Ask for Roger's Soda." When the waiter brought it, two ice cubes bobbed on its fizzing surface. I started to remove them, then dropped the spoon, thinking, what do I care if the water is contaminated? First, Simon, now, Anil. I drained the glass, put it back on the table. My vision cleared. We finished the rest of the meal in silence.

Not uncomfortable silence. There just wasn't anything to say.

Dinner was at the guest house, hosted by Mina's family. She was wearing a fig-coloured sari, her thick curly hair tied back in a plait, a garland of white zai flowers hanging in a bunch from the topmost braid. We hugged and she barely got a chance to introduce me to Ravi when they were approached by another guest. "Gita," she called out to her sister, before she moved away. "Look who's here."

"Shaila! So glad you could make it. Look at us spinsters," Gita smiled. "So beautiful, yet no one will have us!"

"What do you need a husband for?" I asked. "I hear your travel and tourism business is flourishing!"

"Yes," she replied. "But a husband is like icing on the cake, don't you think? Come and meet everyone." I assured her I was quite all right on my own, but she dragged me around anyway, introducing me to a host of cousins, aunts, uncles, and friends. After a while, I extricated myself from a laughing knot of relatives and stood in the corner in front of a large pedestal fan.

After we came back from Banff, Simon called home and told his parents about the job he had accepted in Calgary.

"They want me to go to Halifax," he said, after putting down the phone. "My father has spoken to someone at Mount Allison and apparently there is an opening for me."

"So, why didn't you tell them that *both* of us need jobs and it's no good just you having one." I hadn't met Simon's parents. I'd spoken to them a few times when I'd answered the phone in his apartment. They'd seemed distant, reserved.

"I should have. But I know them, Shaila, they're not going to let up until I've checked out this job. Besides, it's a year since I was home. I think I should go before making the Calgary decision. Even if it's just to rule Mount Allison out."

I sat on his bed, staring at his pillowcase covered with tiny knots. "I thought we'd agreed on Calgary, Simon," I said.

He didn't look at me and went into the bathroom. "Why don't you go ahead?" he called out. "It's not fair that you live in limbo until I make up my mind."

"And what if you decide to take a job out east —" But Simon had already turned on the shower.

"Come here, Shaila," Gita was saying, "and listen to this. Ravi says he's had a change of heart. He's wondering if he's doing the wrong thing getting married. He's wondering whether he should leave Madras for a life of renouncement, in Benares. He won't listen to us. You must entice him to stay, make him understand that paradise is here, with my sister!" She was laughing.

"Stay, Raviji, stay. My uncle will give you a brand new Mercedes," a cousin said.

"With goldified steering wheel and red leather seats," a fat-cheeked boy called out, racing around the room. "Vroom, vroom, vroom . . ."

Mina was looking at me, her eyes shining. I winked at her. "We'll give you a pair of diamond cuff-links," I said to Ravi, "to match the sparkle in Mina's eyes."

"Yes, yes, why not?" Mina's mother said. "And Papa will give you a share of his coffee estate and I will give you all the mangoes from our mango trees."

"And I will make sure that you have never-ending supply of chutneys and pickles!" Akka, Mina's grandaunt, said.

"And I will feed one thousand poor when the first child is born," Mina's grandmother said.

"And I will deliver that first," I said, laughing. Mina was blushing.

"Bas! All right!" Ravi said. "I'm convinced. Farewell Benares. Hello Matrimony."

"Not yet, Mr. Hero," Gita laughed. "You'll have to wait till tomorrow morning."

"Add fifteen hours to that for the real stuff," another cousin guffawed.

It was midnight by the time we returned to the hotel. I turned off the air conditioner in my room and opened the window. The sky was studded, the moon so luminous, so near, so unlike the cold, distant, shrouded object that had dangled aimlessly throughout that last month in Winnipeg. There was a knock on the door. It was Anil. He entered, shutting the door behind him.

"Is there anyone else?" he asked, without much ado.

I shook my head.

"Is it all right, then?"

"You're engaged, Anil. We shouldn't —"

"But remember how it used to be between us? We should be together," he said, stroking my neck. I reached up and touched his face.

November, I walked into Simon's apartment and placed in his fridge some mulligatawny soup I knew he loved; I hadn't seen him since he'd returned from Halifax the previous week, but we'd spoken on the phone. Mount Allison hadn't worked out.

When I came out of the kitchen I noticed how different his apartment looked. The bed was made, the pillowcase was new, the star-gazing equipment that had been sitting idle since he'd finished his research was dusted and propped up, the telescope facing inward. His desk, once strewn with pencil sketches of solid objects and boxes, held a single snapshot of a woman with golden hair. I placed his apartment key on the desk and left.

Mina and Ravi were seated on the floor next to each other in front of the ceremonial fire when we entered the marriage hall the next morning. Listening to the priests singing their rhythmic chants, I felt an odd kind of serenity even though the festive atmosphere was anything but serene. Children chased one another, stuffed hungry mouths with pedas and bondas, played hide-and-seek between chattering guests.

Afterwards, when the eight of us Woodlands Hotel residents were slumped in the front lobby, Neena, Mina's friend from Bangalore, took me aside and asked me to accompany her to an appointment with an astrologer. She didn't know Madras well enough to catch a taxi alone, she explained.

The reception wasn't until six that evening. If I spent the afternoon in my hotel room I knew that Anil would come by. The night before had been nice, but felt more like an ending than a beginning.

"Sure, I'll come with you," I said. "But we had better change out of these wedding clothes."

I went to my room and pulled on blue jeans and a kurta. There was a knock on the door.

"Got to go, Anil!" I said, brushing past him. "See you later."

"Where are you rushing off to?" he called after my back.

In the taxi I asked Neena who we were going to see. "The wand-lady," Neena said.

"The wand-lady? Does she have a name?" I asked.

Neena shook her head. "Don't know. Never thought to ask my mother-in-law."

"Do you consult astrologers often? I mean, do you believe in them?" I asked.

"My husband is having some business difficulties," she replied. "First we thought it was a teething phase. But they've gone on longer than expected. Anyway, since I was coming to

155

Madras for Mina's wedding, my mother-in-law said, why not ask wand-lady."

The taxi pulled up outside a large residential compound. Its tall iron gates were open and as we walked towards the entrance, a chowkidaar came and blocked our path. Scrutinizing us with sleepy eyes, he pointed to a side door.

We knocked. There was no answer. Neena tried the handle. The room was empty except for the bright, colourful pictures of myriad gods and goddesses — some framed, others torn out from calendars — decorating white-washed walls. Sandalwood joss sticks burned aromatically in one corner. Mentally saluting the religious pictures, I looked at Neena. She raised her eyebrows and called out something in Tamil. A stout lady entered through an inner door. The wand-lady.

Without acknowledging us, she sat on a cane mat at the far end of the room. Heavy gold necklaces hung down to her waist, thick gold bangles encircled plump wrists. Above her hung a picture of Ganapati, the words "Remover of Obstacles and Bringer of Good Luck" arched over His elephant head.

Patting a cotton dhurrie in front of her, she looked at Neena and told me in heavily accented English to wait outside, under the jamun tree.

Simon phoned me the next day. "Thanks for the soup," he said. "How come it wasn't yellow this time?"

"I ran out of tumeric," I answered, swallowing hard; my voice was trembling. "Did you both enjoy it?"

"There was no one else with me —"

"I saw your apartment, Simon. I know something when it's staring me in the face."

"Shaila, we should talk," Simon said.

"So, talk. I have lots of time."

"I'm sorry —"

"So am I." The tears were running down my face.

"It's not you. You are not the reason things didn't work out. And I can't say it's exactly me, either. You have no idea how much you mean to me —"

"If it's not me and if it's not you, Simon, then what is it?"

"I don't know, Shaila. Perhaps it's an East-West thing. You read the spaces and I see the stars."

"Shaila! I've finished." Neena came towards me.

"You're smiling! Good news?" I said.

"Yes!" she said gleefully.

"Do you think the wand-lady will see me?" I asked, my words shaping my thoughts.

"Of course. There's no appointment formality, you know. Go on," Neena said. "I'll wait here for you."

When I re-entered the room, the air was thick with the aroma of sandalwood and smoke, the joss sticks had burned down to their last inch. The wand-lady was arranging the folds of her sari. When she looked up and saw me, she smiled. I went and sat opposite her as I had seen Neena do. Up close, her dark mahogany skin was smooth and shiny and, although her teeth were stained from catechu and lime paste, her smile was beguiling.

"What will you want to be knowing?" Her voice was delicate, soft.

"Nothing in particular," I shrugged. "I don't know. Everything, I suppose!"

She reached into the voluminous folds of her sari and pulled out a wooden stick a foot long and an inch in circumference. It was capped at one end by yellow ivory and a silver thread was entwined around its length. She reached for a small pouch on the mat beside her and shook out several medium-sized cowrie shells which she proceeded to cast on the ground. She studied their pattern briefly and, touching my right palm with her stick-wand, spoke nonstop for the next ten minutes. Casting and recasting her shells, she related in a sing-song voice details from my past with such accuracy that I felt she must actually see all of us: flickering, tangible images on her mental screen. Mum, Dad, Simon, me — our physical attributes, temperaments, strengths, weaknesses, professions, relationships.

"What will you want to be knowing now? About future?" she asked, finally.

But before I could answer, she was casting her shells again.

She looked up at me. "This boy in Am-rica —"

"No, Canada."

"I think so he knows you are not being happy in Can-nada because you are needing your people, isn't it? That is why he is telling you go back home."

I didn't reply.

"I think so there is someone here, in Made-ras?"

I nodded.

Touching my right palm with her wand, she shook her head. "This boy, that other boy, no permanent thing, isn't it? Both, simply experience in life. You are being sensible about matters of heart therefore all worries behind. No cause for nervousness-doubt! From now on, everything will be right."

My cynical side told me that she was making such ridiculously generalized statements that I shouldn't believe them. And yet, what she was saying made perfect sense. That there would be nothing permanent between Anil and me I had known all along. As for Simon, that was over.

The wand-lady returned the cowrie shells to her pouch. I reached over and dropped two hundred rupees into a strong box next to her and she beamed at me. At the door, I glanced back; she was opening the lid, reaching in.

Neena was sitting on the grass outside. "Isn't the wand-lady something else?" she said as we walked towards the main road in search of a taxi. "She even described a small, fish-shaped mole my two-year-old has on his left thigh!"

"Neena, do you mind if we make a detour to the Indian Airlines office? I want to find out if there's a flight to Bombay this evening —"

"Aren't you going to stay for the reception?"

"I'd like to go back to Bombay. It's less than a week since I came home from Canada. Haven't had a chance to unpack yet. Besides, I don't think Mina would notice if I wasn't there."

"That's true. The reception will probably have a thousand people. You're going to need luck though, to get a seat last minute!"

After booking my seat at Indian Airlines, I called Mina at the guest house. She was at the hair dresser's, so I asked to speak to Gita and told her I would be leaving that evening. "Is anything the matter?" she asked. I told her what I'd told Neena.

"Mina'll understand, Shaila. To tell you the truth, I don't think she'll remember tomorrow all the people she's met this week. But I know she's delighted that you came for her wedding. Give my regards to your parents."

"I will, Gita, I will. You do likewise with your family, and wish Mina and Ravi all the very best from me. And Gita, don't forget to get in touch any time you're in Bombay!"

Next, I phoned Anil in his room. I told him I was speaking from the hotel lobby and was dying for a genuine Mysore decoction. Did he want one?

As I waited for him in the open-air coffee shop, I looked at my watch. Another couple of hours and I'd be on the plane again.

Anil was taking his time so I ordered two Mysore coffees. When I opened my wallet to pay, the Ganapati locket Mum had given me at Bombay Airport fell out of the change compartment. I quickly looped the chain around my wrist.

Anil came and sat across from me. As we sipped thick coffee, I told him I was leaving that evening. He nudged my foot under the table. "Maybe things will work out for us in our next lives!"

"Maybe," I said, looking at tall Ashoka trees lining the driveway like arrows reaching for the sky.

GLOSSARY

amti	curried lentil soup
asthi	bones
attar	perfume
baday	big
badmaash	rascal
barfi	milk fudge
besan	chickpea flour
bhajan	devotional song
bhaji	curried vegetable
bidi	Indian cigarette wrapped in leaves
biryani	curried pilaf with meat
Bishi	an arrangement where members contribute to a general fund and draw from it on a monthly basis
Bollywood	Bombay's Hollywood
bondas	potato fritter
brinjal	egg plant
catechu	resin collected from a tree
chandrakor	crescent
chapati	flat, unleavened bread made of wheat
chappals	leather sandals
charpai	four-legged cot
chatai	cane mat
chickoo	sapota (kiwi-sized, brown fruit)
chikki	nut brittle
chowkidaar	gate man
churidaar	Jodhpur pants
devghar	a room or a part of a room where gods are housed
dhurrie	cotton mat
dombari	migrant street acrobat
dosa	rice and lentil pancake
dupatta	long scarf made out of thin material

Durga	Hindu goddess
ekdam	too much
garam masala	pungent blend of spices
gauti kadha	hot drink made with lemongrass and herbs
Gayatri Mantra	prayer to the Sun God
gule poli	unleavened bread made of jaggery
haran	deer
Huzoor	sir
idli	rice cake
idli-sambar	rice cake with vegetable curry
jameendaar	landlord
jamun	purple fruit
Janata, janata	a political party, the general public
kadhi	curried buttermilk
Kanjeeveram	a town in Tamil Nadu State
karanji	pastry with sweet coconut filling
Kasa kay. Theek?	How is it going?
khadi	handloom cotton
kheer	sweet milk with vermicelli preparation
kohl	antimony
kokum saar	coconut curry with sour kokum fruit
kothimbir	coriander
kurta	long-sleeved cotton shirt with Nehru collar
Kuthay ahais ge?	Where are you?
ladoo	round sweetmeat
mali	gardener
mangal	inauspicious star, Mars
mangalsutra	black-bead and gold necklace worn by married women
masala	mixture of spices
mirchi masala	exaggeration
MLA	Member of Legislative Assembly
mochi	cobbler
mogra	white variety of jasmine
mulmul	very fine cotton
naka	corner
namaskar	Indian greeting with hands joined together
nashta	breakfast
nayvidya	sweet offering to the gods
pada	village

pallu	end of sari which hangs over the shoulder
pancha	thin cotton towel
pedas	pastry made with condensed milk
phalwali	fruit vendor
phulkari	Indian embroidery
pohay	curried flattened rice
Pothi	Hindu book of prayers
puja	a religious service where offerings are made to God
puri	Indian deep-fried flat bread
Rajdhani	express train between Delhi and Bombay
razai	duvet
salwar-khameez	long shirt and pants worn by men and women
sambar	South-Indian lentil curry
samosa	deep-fried savoury pastry
shaligram	a black, stone symbol of Lord Vishnu
shehnai	Indian wind instrument
shendi	long tuft of hair at crown of head
shevanti	yellow chrysanthemum
shikeykai	Indian herbal shampoo
shrikhand	sweet yogurt dessert
surmai	sun-fish
tabla	Indian drums
tabalji	person who plays the tabla
tadi	fermented alcoholic palm drink
tambora	drone instrument
toba	don't talk about it
thumri	Indian semi-classical song
vaidya	physician
vati	small bowl
vili	sickle-shaped mounted knife
zai	small, white sweet-smelling jasmine flower

ACKNOWLEDGEMENTS

Thanks to the Explorations Program of the Canada Council; to the Sage Hill Experience and Ven Begamudre. I am indebted to my editor, Martha Sharpe, for her searching questions combined with an instinct for ferreting out interesting answers. And thanks to Esta Spalding for her trust and support.

Thanks to Carmelita McGrath for getting me started; to the Nagpurkar family for providing me access to their computer night and day; to all members of the Newfoundland Writers' Guild, Janet Fraser, Helen Porter, and Mary Barry for their individual and collective wisdom; to Julie Brittain for her encouragement and savvy; to Janet McNaughton and Michael Wallack for answering numerous computer crises with utmost promptness; to Michelle Hickey and Donna Dwyer for their many kindnesses. And, as always, thanks to Prafull, Leena, and Rohan for their enthusiasm and understanding.

Some stories have been published in different forms in *Canadian Fiction Magazine*, *Antigonish Review*, *Grain*, *Toronto Review of Contemporary Writing*, and *The Malahat Review*. Many thanks to the editors of these publications.